BREATH
TAKEN

Amanda Jaeger

TABLE OF CONTENTS

DEDICATION

Self-awareness is a tricky thing.
Even when you think you see yourself clearly, it's never through crystal glass.
For you, reader. May a piece of this story clean some of the smudges for you.

PROLOGUE

Amy Jones pulled out another dripping water bottle from her cooler and handed it over to her neighbor, Richard Teft. "Here you go, Richard. Drink up! It's a hot one today. I don't want anyone to get dehydrated."

Truth was, she didn't want to see *him* dehydrated, especially. There was something about Richard Teft that made her stomach flutter and her heart pitter patter, but she had to keep those feelings hidden away from the world. Especially her husband.

So, she focused on her mission without letting anyone know she was watching the condensation cling to Richard's wrist and arm, licking a trail of his skin clean in the summer heat.

At twenty-five, Amy was determined to provide and nurture a group of people who looked after each other. She needed to be needed; to be the nuclear center of a well-meaning community. She needed to provide for the people around her, make sure they were healthy, safe, taken care of. Yet, as she looked at the dark haired man in front of her, it was never enough. She always had to push harder, prove her worth.

How else would she catch the eye of the man who took her breath away?

It had taken a few weeks to convince Laurel at the Bridgewell apartment office to throw together a block party barbeque, but Amy beat her into submission with kindness. Enough award-winning smiles and she could prove to her neighbor two doors down that she was what every man wanted.

She and her husband, Neil, had only lived in number 76 for a few months, and that was all the time it took to feel like this was supposed to be her makeshift family to take care of. The couple with the dogs that never stopped barking were like the loud cousins who always dropped by unannounced. Gladys next door was the grandmother who smelled like smoke and leftover pickles. And Richard was… well, he was Richard. He was too mysterious to be a weird uncle and too hot to be considered brotherly.

Richard was more like the quiet handyman you couldn't wait to watch service the pool shirtless and sweaty. Only, there was no pool at Bridgewell. And Richard worked more with tree climbing gear and saws than hoses.

"Thank you." Richard's dimpled smile drew out the butterflies in her stomach as he pulled a couple of blue floral sprigs from behind his back. They stuck out of his fist like a child's hand picked bouquet. "Lavender. Your favorite, right?"

How did he remember? She had told Neil a thousand times that her favorite flower, scent, and color was lavender. And yet, anytime Neil had offered a bouquet it was whatever was on sale at the grocery store. Usually wilted daisies or roses. While the secretive neighbor presented her favorite without any effort at all.

Amy wiped away the condensation leftover from the chilled water bottle and accepted the flowers in her free hand, tucking them behind her ear. They smelled like comfort and protection; the perfect combination that would soothe her heartbeat from exploding from her chest. "Thanks, Richard. These are fantastic. I keep trying to get Laurel to let me plant a few more of these around here. I think they'd liven things up a little, you know? Invite the pollinators around more often."

She watched his cheeks flush as he nodded. The look Richard gave Amy reminded her of the way Neil used to look at her when they were kids — full of hot embarrassment and repressed butterflies. It was as if a tangle of words would spill out if he were to open his mouth.

She wished Neil still looked at her like that. She wished her insides still fluttered with excitement every time her husband threw her a wink or a nudge. She wished she didn't automatically cringe whenever he playfully pinched her sides or grabbed her ass. They weren't even thirty and yet their relationship already felt like it had aged out of itself.

It wasn't always so dull. As kids, they'd make plans to sneak out of their houses and meet in the middle at the big knotted oak tree. As they grew up, she marveled at how strong he became, with the ability to lift her over his head and up into the branches of that same tree. That was where she watched him etch their initials into the crooked roots that poked out of the soil.

Now, as adults, he mindlessly tagged along in everything they did. It always took an extra nudge and ten more reminders for him to remember their plans. Scratch that — her plans.

"Do you have anything else you're doing this weekend, Richard?" Amy breathed in the lavender and mentally crossed her fingers. Hopefully, Richard would say no. Then he could be at the food drive with her and Neil. And she'd be able to show off her skills in packing heavy boxes *just right* so people could bring them home and feed their families.

It sure wouldn't hurt to have eye candy there.

Richard shrugged. "I'm supposed to go help out my mom sometime soon." He adorably tripped over the words spilling from his mouth. "She needs some help with a few things. A lock, I think. She says the front door opens too easily. A door-to-door solicitor almost helped himself into her house the other day." He shrugged again and drank from the water in his hand. "Almost."

Of course he was going to help his mother. Her butterflies flipped their little wings in fast little circles. "That's sweet, Richard. I'm glad you can help her out." Hopefully, the disappointment in her voice was well hidden behind the adoration she felt.

He gave her a weak smile and rubbed the back of his neck. "Yeah, I'm hoping I can do that soon. It's been on her to-do list for a while. I just haven't gotten around to, you know, actually doing it yet."

Richard was being modest. He didn't want to show off for her, and that made her butterflies pitter patter even more. And even though she wanted to pry into his life and all the ways he took care of his mother so she could daydream of the ways he could take care of her, something else came out of her mouth when she opened it. "You should try Laurel's chicken barbeque. Everyone is saying how good it is." She imagined licking the sauce out of his dimple. "I think it even got a smile out of Gladys."

"Did I hear you say my name?" The old lady made her way across the grassy knoll behind the apartments, swatting the flies away as she passed the trash bins filled with beer cans and leftover takeaway boxes.

"Oh. Hi, Gladys. I was just telling Richard how much you were enjoying the barbeque." Amy's eyes drifted to Gladys's fingers. There were tiny crusted rivers of barbeque sauce embedded between her wrinkles. Disappointingly, the dimple-sauce daydream was wiped clean.

"I'd enjoy it more if there were some more interesting people." Gladys drew from the cigarette dangling from her lips. A wisp of smoke wriggled out and created an ashy cloud between them. "You know, someone who might actually tell me what's going on outside our Bridgewell walls. There has got to be some good stories hiding in someone. Something that'd be worth a dime to listen to." She gestured to the small group around her. "But all these people insist on being dull and boring. One day, someone's gonna give me something good."

"Water, Gladys?" Amy coughed away the secondhand smoke as her hands scrambled at the cooler for a new water bottle.

"Nah. I'm okay, Amelia." She banged on her chest to force out her own cough. "I've got to make my rounds. See what's going on with the good people in this corner of Samhale. See if I can get them to let their secrets out."

"Oh, please call me Amy. Amelia sounds too formal." Her full name always made her feel more distant from people. And with Richard right in front of her, Amy didn't want to feel distant at all. She wanted to feel close, important, as needed as the sunshine itself.

Gladys coughed again. "Yeah, sure sure, Amelia."

Richard gave Gladys a small, crooked smile. It was like he wanted to be polite to this old woman by not coughing out the crap she was blowing into everyone's face. Amy adored him all the more for it.

And, in return, Gladys wiped the corners of her mouth. The barbeque sauce in the creases refused to budge, no matter how much she licked her fingers and rubbed them across her face. "I'm sorry, Richard. I hope I didn't interrupt something here?"

Amy could feel her own skin grow hot as she watched the skin on Richard's neck turn red. "No, Gladys. I was just getting some water."

Her heart slowed down as she watched his every movement after that one by one. His hand reached behind his neck to scratch it. His mouth pulled into something between a smile and a smirk. His left dimple snuck out and winked at her. He stretched his arm up as he scratched further down, nearly reaching his shoulder blade. The simple motion contracted his muscles in powerful knots that begged to be touched, and she drank in every inch.

A touch on her hip broke her from taking in visual gulps of Richard. "Hey, you."

It was Neil, her husband. The man she chose to marry. The shell of the boy she had fallen in love with years ago. "Did you offer to bring the neighbors on the corner something for their dogs? I know they wanted to keep them at a distance so they wouldn't jump all over everyone's plates."

"Yes. Of course, dear."

"And did you go around to collect everyone's trash?"

"Of course I did." Amy could feel Neil's eyes tear into Richard's. "Hi," he eased out in a hiss. "Robert?"

"Richard," Amy whispered to her husband. She scooped her arm around his side. She might as well put on the lovebird appearance. No one wanted to be around a Debbie Downer who doesn't even want to be around the person she married. "He was just telling me that he's going to spend some time at his mother's house this weekend. Help her out with a few of the chores. One of the locks is broken and she's afraid someone is going to break in without trying. Do you think you could help him with that?" She felt her throat tighten as her voice lifted at the end of the question. Why was she asking her husband to help the man she'd rather be with?

Because that's what good people do. They help. And we are good people, she answered herself.

The smile Neil gave back to her didn't feel like it reached his heart. "Sure, I could help. But don't we have Habitat for Humanity this weekend?"

"That's next weekend. Tomorrow is the food drive. And you're right; they do really need us there, don't they?" Amy screwed up her nose. She needed to calculate a better calendar plan. Fill it up with things to do for others to fill herself up. To prove her worth. Catch the eye of the man she eyed.

Richard interjected, the flush in his cheeks now gone. "That's okay, really. It's just a lock. I think I can handle it."

Amy swore that left dimple winked at her again.

"See? He's got it all taken care of."

Amy could feel Neil's chin rest on the top of her head as he pulled himself closer. His chest pushed her forward when he took a deep breath in, no doubt inhaling the perfume of lavender so close to his nose. Protection. Comfort. It tickled when he let it out slowly, his breath blowing strands of her hair against her ears.

Then, a new idea hit Amy. "I have the day off on Wednesday. I saw a post on our community board. There's a pig lady that needs some help at the community center."

"A pig lady?" Richard coughed out this response, the words straining from his vocal chords like raspy notes that could barely fill the air.

And yes, she knew. The idea of a pig lady sounded nuts. Just nuts enough that Richard would take the invite. Who could resist coming out to an event where the main attraction was a couple of pigs named Porky and Piglet? It was too cute not to say yes to.

"A pig lady! She owns a few therapy pigs and hosts community events where people can stop by and interact with them. I bet it will be a lot of fun! I'm going to put our names on the volunteer schedule. We can make it a regular thing!" She noticed Richard was holding his hand to his chest. Was he feeling his own breath going in and out of his lungs? She imagined her hand resting on his chest instead, his chest contracting slowly up and down, and managed an, "Are you okay, Richard?"

The flush came back to his cheeks. "I'm fine," he coughed out. "Just, needed to catch my breath a little."

Me, too.

At that same moment, Amy felt Neil's chest catch his breath. Her hair didn't tickle. His breath was caught mid-inhalation, and she wondered if he could feel the electric butterflies reacting to the sight of Richard in front of her. "Hey, Neil. How about you? Are you okay?"

Air sputtered out of his mouth. "Yeah. I just needed to catch my breath, too."

CHAPTER ONE

"Momma?" Richard Teft knocked again on the front door. He checked his phone one more time. The last text message stared back at him as if waiting for his next move. It was his own — **I'm on my way.**

"Momma!"

His brows furrowed, trying to figure out why she hadn't answered. Her car was in the driveway. He had confirmed plans to visit just the day before, and yet there was still no response from her. It wouldn't be like Emily Teft to ignore her only son's arrival, not when she knew he was coming.

Richard twisted the door handle and pushed it forward with ease. He shook his head. The front door lock had been broken for too long. Anyone could have welcomed themselves in just as easily as he was walking in now, steal her silverware, pocket her jewelry, or swipe her T.V. if they were bold enough.

"Hey Momma! I'm coming in!" He cringed at his own voice, knowing how many times he had startled her in the past smack dab in the middle of a crocheting session.

"Each stitch is important. If you miss one, the whole thing is off. Then all the other stitches have to make up for the mistake, trying to stretch themselves to do a little more than what they're supposed to."

Just one of Emily's life lessons she'd pass on every time he interrupted her. Then, she'd stop counting all together and tell him how it would apply to him. People depend on him to do his part, no matter what his part is.

Garlic. Onion. Tomatoes. Something was burning in the kitchen. Already at 3:00 in the afternoon. Somewhere between one meal and the next. At least that was true for most people. In fairness, Richard's mother used to always invite him over for 4:30 dinners until he finally got tired of eating at a time of day that was meant for locking himself in the bathroom and thinking about Amy Jones. 8:00 paper plates on the couch was more his style.

The plastic bag he had been holding in his hand dropped on the kitchen counter as he turned the corner to address his mother by the stove. "Hey, Momma, you know dinner isn't for another—"

Except, Emily Teft wasn't there. The only living thing in the kitchen was a pot of bubbling spaghetti sauce. It popped and gurgled, splattering the beige backsplash in sticky red polka dots. He wiped it with his hands, spreading the tacky red sauce over his palms and fingertips. He cleaned it off on his pants, and now he felt covered in it.

"There is no one perfect spaghetti sauce. The only perfect sauce is the one you share with the people you love."

The burner knob clicked off at Richard's gentle touch. "Hey, Momma, you left the stove on again." Thank goodness for the broken lock to let him in or she could have burned the house down.

He allowed his eyes to circumvent the kitchen island while he waited for her to answer. She didn't. The only sound was the subtle hum of the stove resting to a cool and the sauce calming down from its boiling fit.

She was probably asleep.

If that were the case, then it was time to quietly fix the lock and get out of there. Let her sleep and wake up to a door she could actually lock.

He lifted the plastic bag from the counter and allowed the contents to fall out: a screwdriver, a pair of screws, and a replacement lock. With all the materials in hand, Richard made his way out of the kitchen, passing the hallway that led to the bedroom. Tipping his toes across the hardwood floors, he hoped he wouldn't wake her.

Another step, and the bedroom light caught his peripheral vision. Emily never napped with the light on. She wasn't asleep after all.

His heels dropped to the floor. No need to be quiet anymore. "Momma? I'm here to fix your front door lock," he called out.

He passed the study on his left where he remembered a piano used to sit, untouched, when he was a child.

"Even if you're playing at the proper tempo, if you don't do it with correct form, it's going to be sloppy. Learn how to do things right."

He took a step past the bathroom on his right that still had stickers that had dried and congealed to the paint on the door.

"Just like stickers, words will leave behind an impression. Be careful where you place them."

Another step and his view stopped his feet in their position. His hands forgot what they were doing, and the handful of hardwear clinked on the floor in an offbeat rhythm.

"Momma?"

Ten steps in front of him, he saw her familiar hand, wrinkled and knobbly, resting palm-side up in the doorway.

"...Momma?"

Her finger tips curled inward. The bony joints jutted out like little hilltops. He had watched those knuckles dance thousands of times between a string of yarn and across the piano keys. And yet, never like this. Never sculptured in a blue stillness. They were always so pink and lively, ready to make the next move with vigor and intent.

"...Mom?"

His voice caught in his throat as his eyes followed the arm down to the shoulders where he used to lay his head as a young boy after every scraped knee, later when the first girl broke his heart, and far less as he nailed his first job interview and learned how much gas bills really would cost him.

"Oh Momma!"

Richard dropped to his knees and cradled her temples. Instantly, his fingers felt cold. He regretted turning down the early dinners and the daily phone calls. His heart broke into bitter apologies for not fixing the lock sooner. He should have done it weeks ago, back when his mom originally asked him. Before the door-to-door salesman could help himself in and before anything else could happen. Anything like this.

Blonde locks fed between his fingers. Salted tears left his eyelids, soaking into the rough stubble on his chin. The cold ran up his hands, through his arms, and into his chest, where it nestled into its new home.

He patted her cheek the same way she used to in order to wake him up when he had slept in, but her hazel eyes stayed glossed over.

"Wake up, Momma! It's time to wake up!"

Tiny red dots decorated the whites of her eyes, painting them in permanent distress. The same eyes that used to cry tears for him in parental despair were now drained of the ability to show any active emotion again.

Richard couldn't be so lucky. His eyes prickled and his throat grew tight. Pools of emotion fled out of his chest; his body shaking every time his heart realized what his eyes were witnessing. Quick waves of grief crumpled his body further and further into a fetal position, wishing he could shrink back into childhood where he could curl into his momma's arms instead of holding her awkward weight in his.

It was so hard to breathe.

"Oh Momma…" It wasn't fair. He could have come over earlier in the day like originally planned. He could have called her more often to check in. He could have fixed that lock ages ago.

A pillow without its case lay above his mother's body. A thought ran through his head so quick, he couldn't grab hold of it to give it much attention: Where was the pillowcase with the stitched lavender sprigs that matched the rest of her sheets? He grabbed the corner of the pillow and with the gentlest touch, rested his mother's head on top of it.

"A pillow teaches us that sometimes at the end of the day, you just need a little comfort."

He positioned her arm down, across her abdomen. She looked more comfortable, like she was in a permanent sleep as opposed to splayed out in all directions on the floor.

The lock.

With placid eyes, he made his way down the hall, kicking the jilted lock he had dropped.

The heavy reality hit him. Gripping the cold metal in his hand, he stormed to the front door, his other hand grabbing the attached knob.

He opened the door. He shut it. He opened it again and slammed it shut. Each time he twisted the knob, he cursed himself for waiting so long.

In a debauched exhale, he threw the lock down, denting the hardwood floor. Richard crumpled to the ground next to it and held his own head between his knees, all of his mother's life lessons ringing through his ears.

"Each stitch is perfect. There's no perfect spaghetti sauce. Play the proper tempo. Leave the right impression."

Heat lifted from the pit of his stomach and rose to his abdomen. Tightening around his lungs, it crept up to his neck and burned at his jaws. He tried to clench them shut to hold back his guttural wail, but it was a failed effort.

"At the end of the day, we all want comfort."

Through breathy heaves, Richard's chest rattled through a series of emotions. When the waves of grief merged into the shadows, guilt swam into his memory. When guilt passed through, remorse crashed into him. When remorse crawled passed, he melted into numbness.

Numbness felt good. This was one he could hold onto.

He didn't think, he just moved. Allowing the fog to wash over him, he drifted back into the kitchen. It still smelled of spaghetti sauce, but his taste buds asked for something else. Something that would keep that foggy feeling around.

He reached above his head, over the refrigerator. The bottles were there exactly as he remembered. Bottles full of brown and golden liquid lined up like little soldiers ready for battle.

Richard grabbed two.

Time to suit up, boys.

He slunk to the floor and twisted off the cap of one. His tongue welcomed the smoky sweetness. He drank it in gulps, allowing it to take over him completely. Each pull of the bottle brought him closer to forgetting what he just saw and who he had just lost.

Richard's phone buzzed and for a moment, he thought maybe he was finally getting the response he had been waiting for.

No such luck. It was Amy Jones, the actual sunshine of Samhale.

Amy: **I left you fresh fruit on your doorstep from the farmer's market this weekend. I thought you could use some vitamin C as the months warm up. You know, stock your body up with everything you can before the cold season hits.**

He let the warm thoughts of Amy wash over him. Her hair, her kindness, the golden flecks in her green eyes. Picturing her face numbed him from everything else around him.

Richard didn't remember answering the door to the police. He didn't remember nodding and shaking his head to respond to their questions. He knew he told them about how uncomfortable she looked, but couldn't recall the exact words he used to describe moving her to a pillow.

Before he realized it, Richard was staring at his front doorstep. Just like the text message promised, there was a box of oranges. Full of vitamin C or K or D or...whatever it was. He didn't care. It didn't matter.

Heat rose from his chest and into his cheeks. It could have been from the liquor finding its home in his bloodstream. It could have been the jolt of unexpected personal loss in the day.

But Richard was willing to bet part of his flushed cheeks were due to the fact that Amy left that box there for him. She thought of him. She allowed her rays of warmth to spread to him. The butterflies inside him stretched their wings and flittered around.

He blinked and found himself sitting on the topmost step, mechanically ripping off strips of peel. A few scattered on the porch beside him.

He blinked again and the few turned into a pile.

Another blink and he had a box full of peel-less oranges waiting in purgatory.

The first taste didn't even taste like fruit. It tasted like detachment.

CHAPTER TWO

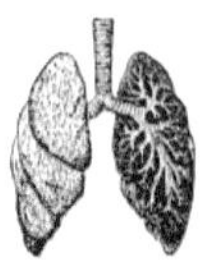

This was not how he imagined his Wednesday afternoon. Standing under a tent, smack dab in the middle of a park, surrounded by sad business employees and two giant pigs. None of his Wednesdays looked the way he thought they would. Or Thursdays. Or any of his days. They all blended together, one giant blur of "Where am I?" and "What have I done?"

Oink.

He clenched his hand to his chest to forcefully regulate his breaths.

Of course, there was only one real reason he was there. There Amy Jones was, holding a leash in both hands, pulling back to keep the 300 pound swine from dragging her in its wake. He half wished it would pull her forward. Toward him. Then he wouldn't have to chase after her at all. She would fall into his lap — into his hands — and she would be his. No fighting or restraining needed.

From the other side of the tent, she smiled at him. He gave her a wave back.

That's right. You enjoy yourself.

Most of the people in the crowd were dressed in khakis and polos — stereotypical carbon copies of 9 to 5 corporate Johns. They had all come together as a work retreat, looking for something to lighten up their spirit, make them feel energized, happy, and ready to show up at work the next day with renewed enthusiasm.

Even if pigs were the magical answer to disparity, what did these people have to be so depressed about? They had both the freedom of a paycheck to put food on the table and the freedom of time to show up on a Wednesday afternoon to pet a stranger's pet pig. From where he stood, they had the freedom to do what they wanted, when they wanted, as they wanted. Their pasted smiles were proof they were happy to skip the middle of their work day to visit with a couple of hogs.

A woman in a red top let out a laugh as the pig sniffed at her pants. "Oh so cute!" she squealed. The sound of her voice sent irritated scratches down his throat.

Cute? Porky wasn't cute. Porky was hoping for a handout. Something soft and squishy to nibble on and gobble down.

He could think of a few things he would like to nibble on right now, starting with those curls he wished he could twist in his hands and pull into his pocket for safekeeping. His mouth salivated as his chest tightened. There was no time to think about that now. The pig in front of him was hungry. The wet slobber spilling out of its mouth was proof all it wanted was food, not a bite of fleshy selflessness standing in front of him.

"Here, try this." And there was the other piece of selflessness. Michelle Fox, the pig lady herself, offered her hand. In her palm was a single baby carrot. Just one. "He loves snacking on these!" Michelle beamed a smile and showed her how to hold the carrot so that the pig would eat it clean off, without taking a chomp out of her thumb instead.

The nameless woman knelt down, offered her palm, and the pig ate it in a single bite. When he sniffed at her some more, she showed him her empty hand. "Sorry, Porky, all done!"

All done. As if this massive pig would be all done with a single baby carrot. Anyone with two eyes could tell that pig wanted more. The same way *he* wanted more. A teensy taste was nothing. You can't get full off one bite. You can't even enjoy it.

And this woman, this Michelle, was teasing the pig, holding out, keeping what he wanted away from his reach and holding his desires hostage from himself. That wasn't fair.

He turned his back to the crowd to adjust his pants without anyone looking.

Damn it.

Furthermore, she was getting this random, nameless woman in the crowd the permission to do the same, too.

Poor Porky.

Oink oink.

I feel you, Porky. I know, infuriating.

Then there was Piglet. Just as round and fat as Porky. Except, Piglet had a black spot around his eye and his grunt made it sound like a growl. He liked Piglet slightly more because of it.

But what he didn't like was the man holding Piglet. The man who hung by *her* side. The man who watched *her* with heart-shaped eyes. Watching him watch *her* made him wish he could scoop *her* up and take her away.

Forever. For good.

The way he wanted.

"Anyone else want to give these two a little love before we have to say goodbye and bring them back to their pens?" Michelle leaned over and patted Piglet on the head. He grunted - *growled* - and she led a few people from the crowd over to them, lining them up like gawkers at a sideshow.

He could tell, she was eating this up. She accepted all the little morsels of everyone around her and all he wanted was one little morsel thrown his way. Just one taste.

Grunt.

Me, too, Piglet.

Amy Jones giggled, and *he* smiled at her for it.

As much as he wanted to, he couldn't have her now. Not with *his* eyes so close. It wasn't her time yet, anyway. But there might have been another option. An option no one else was watching too closely.

"Oh, Piglet really likes it when you get him behind the ear!" Michelle, eager for a response, eager to please, eager for her own pleasure.

His breath hitched in his throat. When these two women stood next to each other, it was as if there was nothing but a glass mirror between them. They were two heads of golden locks. Two manes of unruly curls. Two smiles that sucked up the happiness from others dry, and filled their bodies with it.

He may not be able to have *her*, yet. But there was a pretty good substitution right in front of him. And even more where they both came from. He made a mental note to pay her a visit later. Then he'd have a nibble where he could. Get a taste. Satisfy himself for the moment.

CHAPTER THREE

"There she goes!" The ridiculous yell echoed into Richard's ears, even from inside the closed doors of his white pickup. He took a swig from the warm bottle in his lap and wondered when the liquor store replaced the brown paper bags with black plastic ones.

Outside, white birch pieces fell to the ground. One by one, they hit with a dull thud. With the melody of falling wood playing in the background, Richard shuffled through the collection of plastic bags on the floorboard. The mound of 'Have A Great Day' smiley faces mocked him. There must have been at least a thousand of them, shoved in the pockets of the door, scattered on the floor boards, and making their way under the seats within his cab. They came from gas station stops and hole-in-the-wall greasy food joints, wherever he could make a dollar stretch to shove greasy food down his throat.

He took another swig to let the liquid warm his stomach and gazed out the window with slitted eyes. He was better off without them — all those men in safety suits, chopping down trees for a few bucks in neighborhoods just like this one. Whispering Pass was just another cookie cutter suburban development for residents in Samhale who were better off than Richard Teft. At least, that was what he told himself as he filled himself up with bourbon and resentment.

What would Amy say if she could see him now? Drinking himself away while he stared down the men who still had the job he lost? It didn't matter because Amy wasn't his. Her words weren't meant for him. They should have been saved for that stupid faced husband of hers who didn't know what he had right in front of him.

Another gulp.

Richard watched the group of men gather the wood pieces in their arms to feed the wood chipper. Gobble, gobble, gobble, the chipper would eat it up with greed. He wished he could grab hold of Amy in the same way. Gobble up her arms, her legs, her everything, and melt into her skin so they could become one. He wished he could let her sunshine soak him up and keep him warm.

But the only thing keeping him warm now was his drink.

Within a few minutes, it was nearly gone and so was the wood they were toting away.

As he watched the fuzzy men clean up leftover debris, a little whisper tickled his ear.

Maybe it was his pent-up anger. Perhaps it was the bourbon. But it felt like the whisper was coming from the untouched white oak tree standing behind the crew. He just couldn't make out whatever it was trying to say.

Great. Now I'm hallucinating whispering trees. Ha! Whispering trees on Whispering Pass.

Tick tick tick. A tap on the window, and he had to refocus his bloodshot eyes to the man standing by his truck. He was moving his mouth, but the words were inaudible, like a fish gulping in dry air.

Lazily, Richard tapped the button to roll down the window.

"Dude. You need to get out of here. If the boss catches you…"

It was Dave. Good 'ol Dave, who was always tiptoeing around other people's feelings as if they were crystal.

"Hey, Dave." Richard hiccuped. A short laugh escaped his lips. "Are you talking to the trees, too?"

"Good grief, Richard. How much have you had to drink?" Dave scrunched up his face and took half a step back. "Seriously, you need to leave. Go home and sober up. Maybe after some time, you'll be able to get back to work."

Richard hiccuped again. "As if I want to go back to working under that putz." The last drops of bourbon sloshed from the bottle as he lifted it up to point at an overweight man, watching the other men in hardhats clean around the woodchipper with crossed arms. "He wouldn't know what hard work was if it — hic — jumped up and bit him on his—"

"Richard, you know he doesn't like you calling him that." Dave squinched up his nose as he inched his head through the window. "Look, if you want to sit in your truck and get plastered, that's your call. But I personally think it would be in your best interest to go sleep it off." He let out a long breath. "If I were you, I wouldn't show your face to any of our work sites again until you've cleaned your act up."

And that was that. Dave had nothing else to say. He just walked away as if his little speech was what would save the world of hunger and depression and all the terrible things that crawl into your system and die when grief and guilt dig a hole in you.

Speeches aren't what cure those things. Only sunshine can do that. But the sunshine can't reach you when it belongs to someone else.

The door of the house in front of him blurred into hazy streaks of fire red paint and gold numbers. When was the last time he was at a work site? As a contractor? As someone paid to be on someone else's property?

Oh yeah, it was the last time Puntz *allowed* him to be with the rest of the crew.

"Damn it, Teft! What are you doing?" Richard looked down at George Puntz 'Putz' yelling from the mossy ground. He shook off the verbal scowling and tried to focus his eyes on the cut mark in front of him.

He had cut down thousands of trees before, every kind of species in every kind of setting. He could knock this one out in sections without a second thought. He had secured rope in his sleep and scaled heights in his dreams. This one in front of him was no problem.

"Get the hell down from there, Teft!" Puntz's gruff voice ordered again.

"I know what I'm doing, Putz!"

"Get your ass down here now, you idiot!"

Ignoring the insults, Richard put his hands to work. He finished tying rope around the branch he was about to cut off. His fingers slipped at the last knot, but he finally got it tight. He was sure Puntz was on the ground below, cursing him in mumbled breath.

Richard pulled out his chainsaw from his belt and made the same cut he had made thousands of times before, on the opposite side of the 'v' he had already made in the tree trunk.

As the bark broke, Richard's gaze went to the other side of the tree, planning to watch the section fall safely forward and ease itself down by the ropes he had in place. He'd give his boss a sly smile as proof that he was in the right.

But this time, as the section broke free, so did his knot. It slipped out from the rope and landed on the house's front porch, knocking a hole through the overhang and leaving splintered debris blocking entrance to the front door.

"Shit, Teft. I told you to get down from there!"

Richard adjusted his grip on the tree and as he did, he slipped, too. Panic-stricken, he bear-hugged the tree trunk and felt himself redden in the face.

He could hear commotion below. His co-workers yelled things like, "Move slow and steady," and "get down here," and "drunken fool."

Richard blinked and found himself on the ground, shuffling on unsteady feet. In front of him was a red-faced Puntz. He had no idea how he had landed safely on his feet from the thirty-foot tree.

"Teft, I don't know what the hell you were thinking!"

"Sir, I was thinking I was going to — hic — do my job." Richard's eyelids lazily closed and opened like a solemn wave.

Puntz pointed an angry finger to his safety gear. "Like that?" His finger was shaking at a buckle by the belt.

Richard looked down and saw his buckle was loose. More than that, it was improperly tied. Quickly, he undid the ties and relatched the buckle system, this time correctly. "Like this," he said blatantly.

Puntz shook his head. "That's the third time this week, Teft. Last time, it was a mailbox. This time, the porch. One of these days, you're going to end up hurting someone, maybe even yourself."

An air bubble snuck itself from Richard's gut and loudly erupted into the open. He could taste the leftover bourbon from breakfast.

"Go home, Teft. You're done. I don't want to see your drunk ass around anymore."

Richard screwed the cap back on the bottle and secured it in the passenger's seat, patting the glass lovingly as he adjusted the seat belt around it. He took another lazy look out the window as his ear tickled again. There, the oak tree. He was sure it was calling to him, he just couldn't hear exactly what it was saying.

As he squinted his eyes in an attempt to hear a voice that may have been coming from his head, he saw a figure creeping toward his window. Not creeping. Marching. With fists.

Puntz.

Richard started the engine in his truck and rolled away from the house. Once he reached the neighborhood stop sign, he sped off toward his apartment. He didn't want to deal with Puntz, the putz.

Sure, he'd take some time like Dave suggested, but it wasn't going to be to sober up. He didn't want to stop drinking, and he wasn't sure he could take reality on his own yet. He patted the bottle in the seat next to him. These days, comfort came in the form of liquid and he was happy to access it so easily.

Richard pulled into the Bridgewell apartment complex and sat in his truck to soak in the image of his front door. The number 7 hung rusted on the top panel. There was a faded 8 from where the second number used to be. Another swig of liquid warmth. He should have made the effort to secure it ages ago. But then again, a hanging number wasn't a matter of life and death, was it? Not like a broken front door lock could be. Whether he got to it now or in another few months, it just didn't matter. He would still breathe for another day.

The door to number 77 opened up with a slow creak. Out hobbled a woman with a head full of curlers and a cigarette dangling from her mouth. She took a seat on the rocking chair in the middle of the tiny front porch and breathed in her cancer stick.

Gladys Nightingale. Most chatty women in their eighties were full of stories from their past, but not Gladys. She was full of nosy notions of the entire row of neighbors and judgment enough to seep from her eyes. It was the very reason why she kept to her perch by her front door. She fed her nicotine addiction on her rocking chair so she could simultaneously feed her inner addiction to rumors and gossip.

Gladys waved a hand over to Richard and sat back in her seat. He waved back, with his bottle in his hand. Anyone else would hide it from sight, but his liquid comfort was no secret from Gladys or the rest of the world.

"Richard Teft. How are ya?" Gladys's gravelly voice called from her seat.

"Same day. Same story." Richard waved as he walked up his own stairs.

"Hmm? What story is that?" Her eyes opened wide, ready to soak in whatever he was ready to dish.

Richard waved his bottle in the air.

"I see." Gladys took a long drag and flicked the ash over her knee. "Have you seen Amelia lately?" Her eyebrows did a wriggling dance.

The butterflies inside drunkenly looped figure-eights. Amy Jones was pure sunshine, and the butterflies knew at the sound of her name they could spread their wings and bask in her warmth. Only, he wasn't ready to let anyone know they existed. To the rest of the world, Richard was full of blank stares and alcohol fumes. Butterflies were meant for young lovers and sneaking peeping Toms, and Richard didn't yet fit the bill for either of those titles.

Richard put his bottle to his mouth and allowed it to warm his throat in a giant gulp, putting those butterflies to rest, let them settle to the bottom of his stomach.

It didn't work. As if on cue, Amy and Neil walked out of their door hand in hand. Neil's smile looked comical, forced. But Amy's looked like it could have lit up the universe. Another sneaking gulp, and Richard threw his bottle behind his back. Out of sight, out of mind, out of the sunshine's consideration.

Gladys cocked her head to the side and through slitted eyes called out, "Amelia, Neil," and waved her hand. She was eager to hear stories from someone who may actually divulge their secrets to her, rather than drown them into oblivion.

Neil waved back and slipped into his car. Good. Be gone. Hide away inside a locked sedan so the rest of Samhale could enjoy a little of the warm rays before they had to go back to Mr. Jones and his forced smiles. Amy lifted a finger to tell him 'one minute' and walked over to stand between Gladys's and Richard's front steps.

Richard gulped. This time, liquid-free.

He could almost smell lavender, and the butterflies wanted to inspect the scent, too.

"Hi, Gladys. How are you today?" Her hair was golden silk. Loose curls slipped behind her ear, pushed by a delicate finger with ease.

How Richard wished he could touch the same tendril with the same delicateness, feel it twist and turn through his fingers like liquid gold. He had half a thought to grab the shears in the back of his truck and slice a handful off her head for his personal collection, but in broad daylight, he would be quickly found out. Possibly arrested … if his drunken ass didn't decapitate her with the sharp blades first.

"Just shooting the shit with Richard."

Gladys's eyes narrowed even further, as if she could read Amy's life if she gave it enough concentration. But even though Amy wore her intentions on her sleeve, there was far too much left unsaid about Amy Jones to know her completely. A piece of Richard tied itself in knots, wishing he could have access to any one of those secrets she had hidden from the world.

"I see. How's your breathing? I hope you cut down on those cigarettes like we talked about. That will help with the pain in your chest you mentioned the other day."

And what would help the pain in Richard's chest? The butterflies reminded him Amy couldn't relieve it. Not unless he could have *her* the way his thoughts behind the bedroom door and in the bathroom shower wanted him to.

"Meh." Gladys pulled the cigarette out of her mouth and smashed it into the ashtray on her lap, coughing as she did. "If it hasn't killed me yet, it's not going to."

And the pain in his chest hadn't killed him yet, but it would. Because the butterflies were now pounding his insides, attempting to burst out of his ribcage and force his arms to reach out to grab Amy Jones. He wanted to pull her away from her mister and take her somewhere far away from Samhale, where he was safe to drink her in and *have her*.

Richard turned his back to the women and snuck another drink. The butterflies needed to chill the heck out.

"And you, Mr. Teft..." Richard felt his cheeks flush as Amy's emerald eyes bore into the back of his head, forcing him to turn around and swallow down the fluttering wings. "It's been a long time, hasn't it?"

Richard cocked a smile, hoping it hid his desire and drunkenness. "Um hm."

"I got the feeling you wanted some space since ... well, since what happened with your mom. Again, I am so very sorry for all that happened."

He let his head bob up and down lazily. Of course she wanted to give him space. He purposefully ignored her message of oranges, and all the ones after. Allowing himself to break down in front of her, showing his equal measures of grief and guilt, wasn't an option. She would have felt obligated to take him in, care for him, pay him visits on his couch while cooking chicken noodle soup to feel better.

And if he allowed her to do that, there was no telling what would happen between his hands and her. There would be no holding back, so he held himself back at a distance.

"I know it hasn't been easy on you, Richard." Little flecks of gold on green reflected the actual sunlight from her eyes. They looked bright and sad at the same time, and the sadness tore Richard's butterflies into tiny shreds. "I suppose that bottle of yours isn't full of water, is it?"

Amy knew. Of course she knew. Just because he held a bottle behind his back didn't make her blind or stupid. The butterflies put themselves back together.

She was in tune to his bad habits.

And those golden flecks now reflected disappointment.

"I'll do better, Amelia...Amy. I promise. I'll do — hic — better." And he wanted to make that a true statement. He wanted to do better because she would expect better.

Amy crossed her arms. "I just don't want to see you hurt, Richard. I've seen too much of that, and it makes me feel sick to my stomach thinking about it. If I can help it, I'll do what I can to keep you protected from getting hurt."

It wasn't about him being hurt. That was already done. But if it hurt her to see him hurt? Well, that was too much hurt to go around this corner of town. So he made a promise again, hoping if he repeated himself it would somehow stick.

"I promise, Amelia, I'll do better."

"I told you, call me Amy." She bit her bottom lip when she said this.

But *Amy* felt too close, too familiar, too much like he was taking something that wasn't his. However, if she insisted on dropping the wall of *Amelia* between them, then he'd work on that. Creep in closer by using the closer name.

"I promise, Amy, for you, I'll do better." There. It would have to stick now.

He wanted to say it again as she waved goodbye and joined her husband back at their car, but his voice caught sticky in his throat. He took another pull from his bottle while locking his bloodshot eyes on Neil. Amy's focus was on the car and Richard's focus was on Neil. How he wished he could be in the driver's seat instead, ready to hit his foot on the gas and take Amy to dinner, the movies, a secluded place in the woods where two bodies could share a single blanket and no one could track them by their sounds.

Neil gave Richard a wave as his wife climbed into the car next to them. The two of them were probably on their way to volunteer in the children's ward at the hospital, a floor away from where she would be on paid hours. It was just the kind of thing Mr. and Mrs. Jones would do together on a Tuesday afternoon.

As the car backed out of the parking lot, Richard took another gulp. If he was going to watch Neil Jones drive away with Samhale's finest girl, then he was going to wash away that look with the taste of oaky fixation.

Gladys lit another cigarette. "Careful, Richard. That girl is sweet, but she'll never leave her husband for nothin'."

He fumbled for his door keys. "I don't know what you're talking about, Gladys." The butterflies within him made unsure waves with their wings, and it made him want to throw up.

"Not to say she shouldn't." Gladys blew out a puff of smoke. "She deserves better than him. That's for damn sure." She coughed out a string of smoke. "She deserves something a little more exciting than that quiet schmuck. You know, someone who could liven up this crappy corner of Samhale with a little bit of excitement instead of giving out half-ass waves while keeping a tight-lipped mouth shut." She cleared her throat once more then mumbled, "And I see the way she looks at you, too."

The butterflies stopped moving in Richard's stomach. They hovered, waiting for instruction on what to do with what Gladys just said. But before Richard could calm them down with another pull of the bottle, there was a dull ping that rang from his jeans pocket.

Richard pulled his phone out of his pocket and read the alert message out loud:

Samhale Emergency Alert: Update on public safety in the latest string of home invasion cases. Please click the link to read more information.

"Daggone, another one?" Gladys coughed out a smoky breath.

Richard shrugged his shoulders. "It seems that way." He tapped on the link and immediately, a photo popped up on the screen. A beautiful blonde woman with brown eyes stared back at him. She looked kind, sweet, with the type of smile that encouraged anyone else to mirror it. The name Alisha Smith was displayed underneath with the title 'Habitat For Humanity Volunteer'. He couldn't bring himself to read the entire article, not that he even needed to. He already knew what happened. This was the face of a dead woman staring back at him. Another image he needed to wash away.

Loose notifications had pinged phones and climbed to the top of every social media platform in the past few months. Ever since his mother's dead face had been burned into his memory, the names of dead women plagued Richard's every movement. They were scattered all over the internet, notifying the entire targeted area of the next sad case.

Without another word, Richard helped himself into his apartment and to as much of the bottle his body would allow. The last thing he saw was the woman's face playing against the back of his eyelids. He hated

that she wouldn't leave him in peace. Her smile jeered at his thoughts
until he faded into blackness, but even there, she followed.

CHAPTER FOUR

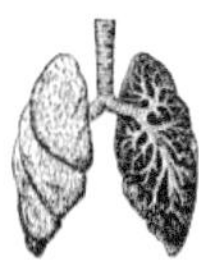

He softly padded his way down the street. A late night walk was always more inconspicuous than driving. At least that was what he had found through trial and error. He got lucky the first time. No one had seen him in the daylight to stop him. He wondered what might have happened if he waited any later in the day. Things would have probably turned out a lot different. He would have never found out the secret to feeling better.

Thank goodness he unlocked that secret for himself and found a better way to handle it. Every time was better than the last. Easier. More exhilarating.

No one was bustling in and out of the suburban neighborhood at this time of night. Nearly every paved driveway had cars parked, in for the night, and every cookie cutter colonial house was settling down with lights out. Only the moonlight lit up the streets just enough for him to read the numbers on the mailboxes.

A smile crept over his face. That was all he needed for a song to wriggle from within him. The lights clicked off in the houses' windows to the tune of the song he hummed to himself.

"Diddle diddle."

As each window darkened with the rest of the scenery, the corners of his lips turned up a little higher. Confirmation this was a much better time to go out. The rest of the world was tucking themselves in for the night while he was awake with passion, counting down the mailbox numbers in his head. 302… 304… 306… 308.

308.

The colonial style house looked exactly like all the others. The only differentiating detail was the bright blue door with a ridiculous wreath made of pages ripped from the spines of books. He supposed it was 'trendy' for people like her. People who liked to be known for one thing in their lives and reinforced it with kitschy pieces in their homes.

He looked around at the neighboring houses. Only a few feet apart from each other, they might as well have been touching. It seemed ridiculous to live in a house that might as well have been sharing walls like a cramped apartment.

Every single one of those might-as-well-have-been-apartment houses had all snuffed their lights out already. That was okay. The rest of the world could go ahead and tuck themselves in. He wasn't concerned about what they'd dream of or how safe they believed their neighborhood was once they were under the covers. He only had thoughts for one person tonight, and she was behind that blue door in front of him with the gold numbers 308 in the center.

The girl with blonde hair and eyes colored with sickening kindness.

The one who reminded him of *her*, though he couldn't have *her*. Not in the way he wanted, the way he hid from the rest of the world. It was his secret he kept to himself, behind closed and locked doors and away in his mind. He couldn't have *her* in *that* way. Not yet, anyway.

Eventually, he would. Eventually, he'd have *her* in every way possible. He'd make sure of it.

A deep inhale and the air hitched in his throat. There it was again, the inability to suck in the air fully. He had to control his shortened, choked breaths to keep from caving in on himself. This hadn't always been the case. He wasn't born with this incapacity to fill his lungs. This was a recent realization he couldn't...wouldn't... accept as reality. The slow grip of suffocation took hold of him over time, and it frustrated him. He needed to break through what was keeping him from breathing freely… from *being* free.

He choked on what air he had as he exhaled. He couldn't wait to breathe normally again, to fill his lungs and not worry about if the next breath would come or not. And now he's figured out a way to make that happen. He was going to take the breaths of others for himself. It was the only way.

And it was the most delicious way.

He knew the exact moment would come when he wouldn't choke on his own air. It would feel like opening a door wide with the air flowing in and out with complete ease. Nothing else could provide that kind of freedom, and it felt exhilarating to know he held that unbreakable power in his own hands.

And yet, he also knew the feeling would end up fading away eventually. It never lasted long enough to be satisfying. Then he would find himself back in this same position: Stalking the night air with a pillowcase in his hands, on the hunt for his next breath of relief. It was a shame the feeling was a temporary reprieve. It wouldn't stick until he was able to have *her*.

Not yet, though. He needed to wait until he was ready.

He zipped up his hoodie, and his hands found their way inside the front pocket. The cotton fabric twisted in his fingers and he was thankful he had the sense to line it with plastic. It took far less time that way, and the quicker his actions, the quicker he could fill his lungs. He kept a hold on the pillowcase in his palm as he made his way toward the side of number 308.

A light went out on a side window, and he took that as his cue to move forward. He'd wait here, leaning against the cool siding of the house, humming to himself until his watch read 10:16 for no other reason than it sounded like a good time for her to be asleep. At least, that was how he had been trained to believe. His bedtime was 10:00. That would give him at least eight hours of sleep, which was imperative for a healthy body, according to *her*.

Most days, he would lay awake for hours, wondering if he could pinpoint the moment when he felt this way. He'd allow his mind to wander from the morning jogs to the weekend barbeques. Somewhere between them, something inside him snapped. No, not snapped. Strangled. Something inside of him had wrapped around his lungs and hung in that position with a relentless force he had to fight against every day.

But on the good days, he fell asleep quickly. The last number he would see on the side table alarm clock was 10:16. The woman in number 308 was definitely not someone who would have to sit up for hours wondering where her life went wrong. Living the healthy suburban life, there wouldn't be anything occupying her mind past bedtime. She was definitely a 10:16 sleeper.

The time passed with his odd sounding lullaby filling only his ears. How he wished he could sing it out for the whole world to hear, but he knew that wasn't possible. Not now, anyway. When he could have *her*, he'd be able to belt it from the rooftops. Until then, he'd make do with his short reprieves. He sucked in what he could in his airways and slipped his fingers under the window's opening.

He looked at his watch and waited for the second hand to march its way to the top. Once it did, a tiny bell went off in his head. 10:16. It was time.

He slid the window open with ease. Chilled air seeped out, even colder than the autumn weather. The feeling rippled from his fingertips down his spine, shocking him into another level of excitement.

With an ear aimed in the direction of the bathroom, he listened for a moment. Nothing. It was still, waiting for him, welcoming him. He eased himself in, landing on the cold tile floor. To his right was a laundry basket and on the top of the pile was a pale blue shirt. Printed on the front was the silhouette of two people and a house — the Habitat for Humanity logo. Perfect. The right house. The right Alisha. The right place. The right moment to steal a breath for himself.

"Diddle, diddle…" he whisper-sung just to himself.

In less than fifteen minutes, his airways would clear and he'd be closer to having *her*.

CHAPTER FIVE

She breathed in the cool evening air, filling her lungs with its deliciousness. The rest of Samhale County might have been folded within their bed sheets, but not her. The open air called to her. It whispered her name and begged her to get up and see what hid after sundown. So she slid her legs through the window opening and inhaled the evening dew.

The damp grass tickled her toes, and she giggled before sprinting to the side of the house where a skateboard and helmet waited. Tennis shoes were stashed in a nearby bush, and she slipped them over her damp bare feet, socks be darned.

Prepping herself for an evening stroll, she turned back to her house. All the lights were off. Check. Mom was asleep. Check. Her window was still open for easy access when she needed to come back. Check.

"So long, suckers," the girl whisper-shouted back at the house. They didn't know what they were missing by sleeping the night away.

She was tired of all the grown-ups talking over her, ordering her every move. "Don't do this" and "Don't do that." What did they know? Nothing. They knew nothing. Either that or they were keeping secrets away from her, which was probably more true.

They did tell her a teensy bit. Apparently, there was some creep wandering around Samhale hurting people. Women, specifically with blonde hair just like hers. But that was it. They wouldn't tell her much else. That was how grown-ups were. They let you know just enough to try to scare you away from doing the things you wanted, leaving you with a thousand questions they refused to answer. Sometimes they treated her like she was an idiot who didn't need to know much else. Little did they know, she would just look for the answers elsewhere.

The grown-ups who had really big secrets thought they could keep them hidden in the dark. She saw through that, though. At night, they couldn't hide their secrets from her anymore. She knew how to keep her eyes owl-wide open to see through it all and find the truth of what everyone hid from her.

Night was when she learned Mrs. Beasley invited a man who wasn't Mr. Beasley into her house. It was when she learned Mr. Boxworth smoked something that smelled funny in his backyard. And it was when she found out Clay, the teenager off Trisdon Street, slept on the front porch if he didn't get home before his curfew. She thought about telling Clay the secret to leaving a window unlocked for yourself. It made logical sense to her, but then again, logic didn't come as easily to everyone else.

Rolling down the street on her skateboard, she touched her own blonde hair that peeked out from under her helmet. Normally, she wore it in pulled-back pigtails or braids. That way, it stayed out of her face and out of her way. But the helmet helped, even without anything tying up her hair. Besides, it was safer to wear a helmet. And she wasn't stupid. She was going to keep herself safe.

Her mom told her last Tuesday they were getting it cut because of the creeper, but she wasn't worried about that. Mom hadn't booked an appointment yet. And besides, if there was a creep wandering around, he wasn't after nine-year-old girls. He was after old ladies, like Mom's age.

And even if he did decide to change his mind and come after kids, she was confident she would be faster than some old creeper on two feet. Probably smarter, too. People were always commenting on how smart she was, and she was always willing to prove it by outwitting the person in front of her. And she was always willing to prove how fast her skateboard made her, as well.

She turned left down Beacon Road, where the neighborhood of Whispering Pass opened to a wider group of houses. Her mom never let her go down this far, not without her eyes on her. She was supposed to stop at the end of her own street and turn around. Come back home by the time *Dateline* was over. But on her nighttime adventures, skateboarding down the extra roads was as second nature as her own front yard. The whole neighborhood was a scavenger hunt for her: little clues to find whatever it was the grownups kept from her.

Beacon Road turned into Clapton, which turned into Rydell. Each of these streets had sleepy homes, no lights on, no movement outside. It seemed that all the secret-keepers were doing their job right tonight for once. She spat on the side of the road. Stupid grown-ups. Mrs. Beasley didn't even have her light on. Mr. Beasley must have been home, preventing whoever that other guy was to show up.

Then she flew down Trisdon, hoping maybe Clay was stirring on his front porch. That might be her only source of entertainment for tonight. Maybe she'd finally show him how to crack the window open just a little to make it easy to slip inside without Mom or Dad ever noticing.

He wasn't. He must have come home early enough not to get locked out. She screwed her nose up in frustration. "Darn it!"

Just as she was about to push herself down the next street, something caught her eye. Movement just across Clay's boring house. Whoever it was thought he was being sneaky. He was wearing a dark hoodie and crouching behind bushes. And, yes, it was a he because he was standing like a he. No self respecting woman would walk around all bow legged and hunched over. That was the kind of thing almost-sneaky people did. Well, almost-sneaky men, that is. Good. It wasn't going to be a boring night after all.

She bent down to the ground and sat behind a mailbox post, holding her skateboard still. Real actual sneaky people did things like normal, but kept an open eye on the stuff around them. Both of her eyes were wide open now, wide as she could make them. She tried her hardest not to blink, in fear of missing the slightest thing. Missing out on whatever this guy was doing wasn't an option. This was going to be a good secret, one that was bound to give her more information than any of the grown-ups would willingly give up.

The man shifted from one bush to another, making a rustling noise she could hear from across the street. He was rummaging his hands in his hoodie pocket, like he was searching for something, but he didn't take anything out. He just stopped his shuffling in place and looked up at the house he was near. Another almost-sneaky person move.

Come on, guy, take the thing out of your pocket so no one knows you're hiding something. And move, for goodness sake. Standing still as a statue while staring inside a house is so freaking boring!

She watched him watch the house until her eyes grew heavy, and she had to hold back a yawn. The whole time he stood still, his back toward her. Her body wanted to leave from this squatting position, but she knew if she was patient enough, something would happen. Whatever that something was, it was going to be worth it. So that was what she did. She decided she would wait a little longer and see what kind of secret this almost-sneaky person had.

Then, he started moving slowly. Her body didn't want to yawn anymore and her eyes opened even bigger than they were before.

This is gonna be good.

He crept up to the house and found a window. He reached out a hand and touched it. Then, backed away. She didn't think her eyes could widen any bigger, yet they did. She didn't even care that they were drying out while soaking in the movements playing out in front of her.

Why the heck did he touch a window and back up?

He moved to another window and touched it instead.

What was different about this window?

His arms slid up, just like hers did when she helped herself back in through her bedroom window. He wasn't a sneaker at all. Her heart pounded like the drum she hid in the corner of her closet. This was a creeper. And she was watching him creep right into this person's house. Oh how she wished Clay was on his front porch so she wouldn't be alone in this. The grown-ups would never believe her if she told them. But they would have to if someone else like teenager Clay saw the same thing.

The window he stood at was now all the way up. She wasn't sure what she expected the hoodie man to do next, but she didn't expect him to pull a piece of fabric from his hoodie pocket.

So that's what he was hiding. Fabric?

That was weird. And with the fabric in his hands, he stepped even closer to the window.

He looked like a spider crawling through it. Arms and legs bent in weird directions. Something about this seemed extra strange. Extra creepy. Like some horror movie monster, except this was real, right in front of her.

This was even more strange than the man that wasn't Mr. Beasley who went to Mrs. Beasley's house late at night. At least he used the front door. And Mrs. Beasley always let him in happily. No creeping around. No spider crawling through a window. He just walked in like he lived there every Thursday night when Mr. Beasley worked late. She always wanted to ask Mrs. Beasley about it, but every time she visited Mom, she wondered if that was the kind of secret that should be out in the open.

Who used a window?

Oh right, she did.

But she wasn't a creeper. She went through her *own* window, and it wasn't weird if it was your own house you were sneaking into. That was just being smart and crafty and getting things done without asking for permission. It was always easier to ask for forgiveness than permission.

But was that true if it was someone else's house? Because this couldn't be the creeper-man's house. If it was, he would have known which window was unlocked the first time. He would have left one unlocked for himself and come back to that one right away. Or he would have helped himself to the front door. That would make more sense. Grown-ups don't have to creep through windows when they owned keys to their own houses.

So this was a spidery-creeper who didn't have a key. This wasn't his house.

A minute went by and nothing else happened, so she decided to creep. No, not creep. She wasn't a creeper. She snuck her way a little closer. To the front door. Knocking wasn't a good idea. It was late enough that her mom had already gone to bed a while ago, way before she left. Considering all the lights were off inside this house, whoever was inside was probably already asleep, too.

Well, except for the hoodie guy creeper-man. He was inside and he definitely wasn't asleep. Maybe it would be a better idea to find out where he went first. The window he spider-crawled into was still open, but following in after him wasn't a good idea. He would probably come out the same way, and if he did, she'd be trapped. Who knows what a spidery-man would do if he trapped her.

The other side of the house had similar windows. All closed. She didn't test to see if they were unlocked. They weren't her windows. This wasn't her house. She knew better.

Something moved inside, but the blinds prevented her from seeing what it was exactly. Just darting shadows. One shadow darted from one side of her view to the other. A second shadow darted, too. Cat and mouse shadow play, only this didn't feel like a game.

Then a thud sounded from inside the house. Something fell. The sound was like the time she dropped her piggy bank on the carpeted floor. It didn't shatter, but its heavy weight made for a loud sound. A boom without a crash.

She thought she heard someone talking, but couldn't make out what exactly they were saying. It was like when her mother talked to her through a closed door, all muffily sounds that didn't make sense. Just like when her mom talked to her in a muffiliy voice, she shrugged. Hard to understand what you're supposed to do when you don't understand words that are being said.

Another couple of thuds. If it were a piggy bank, it probably would have broken by now. Even on carpet, something fragile can't handle that kind of roughhousing; eventually, it would shatter. She knew because her piggy bank did end up breaking after she dropped it again. Twice more, actually. Pennies and dimes scattered everywhere in a metal explosion across her room. It had looked pretty cool.

Whatever was behind these walls probably didn't look as cool.

Then she heard a voice. Clear as could be. No more muffily-ness, even from behind the walls.

A man said, "I can breathe. Diddle, diddle."

And then there was nothing. No movement. No voice. No sound. No nothing. Unless… was that singing?

She looked across the street, hoping for a sign of Clay or anyone. She spat on the ground in frustration. No one was around. And that was that. She was alone in this secret and she had to keep it inside of her now. If she told Mom, she'd just get in trouble for sneaking out. If she told anyone, including Mom, no one would believe her.

This was just a note to keep in her memory piggy-bank so she could compare notes later. She'd be out again, and she'd be looking for the spidery-creeper man or anything else suspicious.

She dragged her skateboard to the street and with a nursery song stuck in her head, headed back down Trisdon, to Rydell and Clapton. She slowed her pace when she got back to Beacon and turned onto Whispering Pass's main street: Coventry Lane.

She passed the old oak tree she thought was haunted and the sleeping houses around it. "Lavender's blue … lavender's green." When she found the blue door to her house, she stopped her board and carried it to the bushes where it would hide until next time when she could scavenger hunt for more secrets. "Diddle diddle."

Though she dropped the weight of the board and helmet, she still felt like she was carrying something heavy with her. She was holding a creeper's secret. Something the grown-ups would never tell her even if they knew, and wouldn't believe her if she said a word about it to any of them. Grown-ups never took nine-year-olds seriously, anyway.

CHAPTER SIX

Light pierced through the broken window blinds. When did he fall asleep? Richard couldn't remember what happened after helping himself back home and kicking off his shoes.

He rubbed his eyes awake, cursing the sun for waking him up. The blinding light wasn't the sunshine he wanted to welcome into his life. The sunshine he wanted he couldn't have.

Too bad he woke up at a time when the rest of the world believed it was too early to start drinking again. As they say, it's five o'clock somewhere.

Groaning, Richard rolled to his side on the worn down living room carpet. This was a good sign. At least he was on his own living room floor, rather than curled up inside a shopping cart in the local Kwik-Mart parking lot. He still couldn't come up with an answer as to how that happened.

It was all part of the same Groundhog Day: Wake, drink, fill up with sorrowful guilt, and crash. Over and over while he daydreamed of what it would be like to fill himself up with Amy Jones instead.

To wake up next to her. Breathe in the lavender in her hair. Wrap his arm around her and soak in her warmth. Spend the day learning every curve of her body instead of reintroducing himself to the curves of his dirty glass.

He lifted himself off the floor and found his phone on his coffee table. 12:15.

His stomach gurgled. Food. He needed food.

In the kitchen, he opened the nearly empty fridge. A jar of old mayonnaise, a few slices of bread, and an expired bottle of orange juice. The breakfast of champions.

He took out a heel of bread for the toaster and poured himself a glass of chunky juice. Giving it a whiff, he figured it was fine. No worse than anything else he became accustomed to putting in his body. While waiting for the slice to toast, he searched for the bottle from yesterday. Fifteen minutes of searching, he finally found it on the floor by the couch, only a small pond of bourbon settled at the bottom. Had he really drunk most of it yesterday? Probably.

He emptied the rest into his orange juice and tossed the bottle in the trash. As it clinked against other discarded glass, he made a mental note:

Check for when the next recycling day is.

Recycling was something Amy would do, and she would forgive him for drinking himself to death if he were helping out the planet.

Amy by the recycling bin. Amy tossing in cardboard boxes of organic grains he couldn't pronounce. Her beaming smile. A wink. Her bouncing blonde curls that hit her bare neck, shoulder, dipping into her cleavage.

Yes, he would have to make sure he'd fill up the recycling bin, too.

His hands were now empty. No more plain toast. Half the glass he poured was now empty. And again, when did this happen? Because he could remember serving himself the breakfast of champions, but he didn't remember tasting it.

While he let his digesting toast soak up what was gone of his sour beverage, Gladys coughed. This was easy to hear, as always. The thin walls in Bridgewell apartments alerted Richard to every movement of his neighbor in number 77. That cough meant she would be outside on her rocking chair stoop within a few minutes, a new cancer stick in hand. He banged on his chest, feeling a chunk of OJ make its way to his intestines. A belch.

Fresh air would do him good, too.

He tossed back whatever was left in his glass and met Gladys, already in her rocking chair perch in a crown of rollers and smoky haze. A real life *Maxine* meme in action.

"Hey, Gladys."

"Richard Teft. Glad to see you facing the daylight."

"That's not fair, now. I was out just yesterday."

"Mmhm. I suppose you're right." Gladys leaned back and took a long drag of her cigarette. As she blew out the smoke, her finger pointed to Richard's mailbox, a small metal box nailed beside the front door. "You slept right through management. Laurel knocked on your door nonstop for fifteen minutes this morning. Bugged the ever living hell out of me; couldn't hear my soaps over the pounding. How am I supposed to know if Jane killed her boyfriend or if it was her evil twin?" She took in another drag. "When you didn't answer, she left something in your box." A shake of her head bounced her curlers like little bobble heads. "A bright pink paper. I suspect it ain't any good news."

Sure enough, a loud fluorescent pink paper stuck out of the box, not so quietly waiting.

A familiar cold washed over Richard. He had seen this before: A late payment warning.

Gladys's chair creaked as she adjusted her weight to get a better look. Nosey woman. She should know better.

"All good, Gladys. I just need to pay Laurel a visit."

That was how it worked before. That was how it would work again. He'd walk a block to the office, dig out whatever cash he had, give her an award winning smile, and walk away.

"Um-hm. Just let her know she interrupted my stories at just the wrong point, will ya?"

Richard hit his chest when his soured breakfast threatened to make another appearance. "I'll make sure to do that, Gladys."

The door to the rental office stuck on its hinges like glue. Richard had to jam his elbow in to encourage it to open, something that took more effort than he had. He breathed in the stale air. Thirty-year-old unwashed carpet and plug-in air freshener: the scent of failure and disappointment. No doubt, the smell would attach to Richard's skin so he could permanently wear it.

Exactly what he needed; something else that would ward away Amy Jones with repulsion.

Richard pulled out his wallet and fished out a handful of cash from inside. It didn't matter how much it was. Cash was cash, and it would pay his way for at least a couple of weeks. He put on his best apologetic voice and slapped the money on the desk. "I'm sorry I'm late again, Laurel. I'll have more for you next week."

Don't forget to smile.

He flashed his teeth, a grin, a slice of charm that won Laurel over every time.

Laurel slid her glasses up the bridge of her nose. "Mr. Teft. Good to see you again." She was a petite woman, no taller than five feet. Her tiny hands made the desk look massive. She held one of them out, and eyed the form in his hand.

He flashed his charm again. Easy peasy. "Oh. Here." And now was the time to carry out the rest of the routine. He'd hand her the form, she'd accept the money, and he would have two more weeks before the next notice would arrive in his mailbox.

And two more weeks where he could safely watch for Amy outside his front door and log everything to memory: the movement of her hips, the way she walked, and the way the sun bounced off her skin because she was too radiant herself to absorb the rays. He'd write it all in the part of his brain that wouldn't get washed away into drunken fuzziness.

And if ever her image faded, he'd watch her again. Absorb her again. Rewrite his memory over and over until it was carved into his consciousness so deep no blackout would be able to erase it.

"Oh, dear…" Laurel shook her head. "I'm sorry. I don't think I can accept this." As petite as she was, when Laurel stood up, her presence took up the entire room.

The Amy-images faded.

No.

Her blonde hair gone.

No.

The lavender replaced completely by the plug in.

No. No. No!

All that was left was Laurel, taking up the entirety of space around him, forcing him to stop thinking about sunshine and focus on that placid room he was standing in.

"Richard, this is an eviction notice."

No. This was wrong. This couldn't have been an eviction notice. This was the same screaming pink form, the same Bridgewell letterhead, the same stupid notice he had handled a million times before.

A million? That may have been an exaggeration. A hundred might have been closer.

"Eviction? No. Here's your money. I'll give you more later. Two weeks, tops. Promise." And that dimple forced its way through on another award-winning charm smile.

"Mr. Teft." Laurel's voice didn't waiver. Neither did her eyes. They both bore into him as if she never knew about their routine deal. But that wasn't true. She always took his cash. She always accepted his dimpled smile. She always waved him goodbye so that he could go back home, close his bedroom door, and feel Amy in his hands.

Yet, here Laurel was, running down a list of reasons why the unspoken agreement between them was no longer an agreement at all. "You've been late on your rent for months now. We've accepted payments toward it in the past, but we can't do that anymore. We've lowered your monthly amount. We're footing your end of the trash utility, and yet each time you're paying less toward the full bill amount. We can't make any more accommodations. In fact, this is the third eviction notice we've sent this month. They've all gone unanswered until now. I hate to do this to you, Mr. Teft, I really do. But, we can't be okay with tenants ignoring their rent. That's just not the way of running things. I'm sorry, but you need to empty your apartment and be out by the end of the week."

The third notice? How had he missed the other two? Surely, he would have noticed the word eviction on one of those angry neon papers, wouldn't he? Then again, he couldn't even remember the last time he bought orange juice. His morning breakfast was proof of that.

Now his mistake? His forgetfulness? His oopsie? Had caught up with him.

He had to be out by the end of the week.

The end of the week. Shit.

That was only three more days. That left Wednesday to watch Amy swing her hips out to shut the car door after a shift at the hospital. That left Thursday to breathe in her hair as she walked past Richard's front steps. And that left Friday to soak in every ounce of her sunshine and burn it into his retinas so he would forever have Amy's nooks and crannies etched into memory.

And then Saturday, he would have to risk it all washing away with a bottle or two or five. Whatever he had left hidden from himself. Saturday he'd have to plead with his demons to keep Amy as a part of him so he could always have sunshine within him.

Richard found himself standing at the bottom of his steps, staring up at the faded 8 on his front door. This was a place to lay his head. But it wasn't home. A roof and four walls, and a place for him to hide behind closed doors and pretend his hands were a little less calloused and a little more feminine. And pretend that Mrs. Jones wasn't a Mrs.

Door 76 creaked open and out walked a head of blonde curls and a body full of curves. The butterflies in Richard's heart jolted alive as his mouth shocked itself dry. The world around him came to a complete standstill, or maybe that was his breakfast booze kicking in. It didn't really matter, because Amy Jones was standing two doors down, so Richard would do anything possible to stop time itself and will her toward him.

Step this way. Just one step closer. No, not toward your car. Here. To me. Let me see you. Get close enough to me so I can touch the silk on your head and taste your sweet scent in the air. Come. Here.

But she didn't. She had her work face on and a duffle bag on scrubs over her shoulder. He knew what she kept in there from months of watching her leave and return from work. A big blue duffle bag meant it was work day Amy. Neil on her arm meant it was volunteer day Amy.

Thank the heavens it was work day Amy. Neil must have been inside, sitting in the dark. Doing whatever husbands did when their sunlight was literally missing.

This way. Just another step over here. You come to me because if I come to you, your husband will notice. And I'll become the bad guy. The guy who snoops on his neighbor's wife and creeps into her world. I'm not the bad guy, Amy. I'm the good guy. The good guy who just wants to be closer. Come. Closer.

"Richard Teft!" Her voice was like butter: soft and velvety. Richard could spread it on toast and eat it for breakfast. For a moment, both he and Amy stood on their front porches and looked at each other with the gap of Gladys's empty steps between them. Her buttery-self was only a porch distance away.

Please, closer, Amy. I can't have buttery toast without butter.

She didn't move closer, but she did move. She adjusted her duffle bag on her shoulder, and it tugged on her shirt just enough to accentuate her neck. Slender. Creamy. A plate of yogurt to the side of butter. Neil Jones was a lucky man. He was always able to fill himself up with a plate of deliciousness, an endless supply of cream and butter.

Had he been quiet too long? Probably. He should have said something.

"Hi, Amelia." That was good, but he needed to include an airy wave. He did. And then he mentally beckoned her again.

Just a little this way. You can go after that. Leave for work. Do what you need to do. But I need you here, first.

"How many times have I told you? Call me Amy," she called back. And she was moving closer. "I see your hands are free. No liquid meal in sight! That's a good thing! Make sure you get plenty of fresh air today. Go for a walk, enjoy the sunshine." Amy held her arms out, palms up to the sky. She was soaking in the sunshine even though she didn't need to because she *was the sunshine itself.* "It's beautiful today. There's no excuse for not soaking in some vitamin D!" Her voice carried like an overprotective songbird he'd never be able to catch.

Closer, Amy Jones. I need to be able to feel your warmth.

Richard sucked in a deep breath. The smell was fading heat off the sidewalk and the autumn air blowing through the trees. But he wanted to smell more. "Yeah, I suppose so."

"What's that? I can't hear you?" Amy moved. She actually moved closer to Richard.

"I said, I already got a walk in today," Richard called louder. And now that he was actually calling her over mentally, he wasn't so sure. She was six feet, three feet, a single foot away. He really could smell lavender in her hair and taste the sweetness of butter in her voice. But without a Gladys buffer…

He clasped his hands together behind his back. There was no telling what they'd do with Amy so close he could taste her.

And if Neil saw…

What was he thinking? If Neil saw, he would be Amy's wingman. He'd hand over a spare vitamin lecture or offer to brew a fresh cup of sobering tea. It was just what the Joneses did. They lent a helping hand. They offered advice. They did everything they could just to make sure the people around them were taken care of.

But the only person Richard wanted to feel the helping hand of was right in front of him. No Mr. in sight.

"Say, Richard…" Amy bit her lip.

Why did she have to do that? All Richard wanted to do was pull that bottom lip out of her mouth and bite it himself. Just a nibble. Enough to taste the sugar it was made of.

"What are you doing tomorrow?"

Now she was close enough he could taste the lavender. He could smell the golden rays radiating off her. And the butterflies inside of him were going insane. They fluttered this way and that, crashing into one another and tangling their wings into knots. It made no sense how that could happen, but that was how they were. Knotted up and tangled as if the butterflies themselves were a ball of twisted yarn.

What did he have planned for tomorrow? Nothing. It was nothing. He had nothing planned for tomorrow.

"Tomorrow?" His mouth betrayed him. That one single word carried out a tone of hope. A hope for plans? To see Amy? To taste her plate of cream?

She nodded. "Yes, tomorrow. There's a food drive at the elementary school up the road. Neil was going to come, but he is taking over a project at the library instead. And Jennifer, who normally helps out, says she has to focus on her garden instead." Amy's eyes broke the butterflies inside Richard. They watered up and reddened, and the butterflies sagged into soggy puddles. "They're just really low on people and we could really use some extra help. The couple of us who regularly go just can't do it all on our own. There are a lot of people who need this food, Richard. And there just isn't enough manpower to make it happen fast enough." She twisted her mouth to the side and furrowed her brows. "Of course, if you can't make it—"

"I'll go." Again, Richard's voice betrayed him. The butterflies scooped up the words and tossed them out of his mouth before he could even think of them. The broken look on her face needed to be fixed, and even though his mind yelled for him to stop, *Amy isn't yours, Richard,* the butterflies scooped more words out of his mouth again. "I'll be there, Amelia."

"It's Amy." And she was sunshine again. Not broken. Not dimmed. Full on brightness and warm rays. "And thank goodness you're going!" Her hands clapped together and Richard felt his name added to the calendar in Amy's heart. "I'll see you at the school at 4:00 PM? That's where we'll be. Right in the bus loop to hand out meals."

"I'll see you then." His own face morphed to match hers. He tried to mimic her brightness, too, but he was still so much duller than her. He could never match to her brilliance, no matter how much of her warmth he felt.

"It's a date!" Amy sent him a wink and a smile that lit up the sky even brighter than the sun itself.

"A date."

He blushed. What a choice of words. Even though it wasn't a candle lit dinner or a movie to snuggle up, this would be a date, right? Maybe not in the conventional sense, but that didn't matter to people like Amy, to people like Richard. Convention wasn't meant for either of them.

He knew they couldn't end up hand in hand, skipping down Lover's Lane. They had things to do. They had people to serve. And Richard would finally be able to show his worth to her.

"Oh shoot." Amy looked at her wristwatch. "I need to get to work. The hospital calls."

And so does fate.

"Treatment can't wait for most of the people in there, you know?"

I'll wait for my treatment after you treat others.

"Make sure you get in another walk, if you can. And if you happen to have some almonds at home, snack on them, too. Often."

Almonds aren't the kind of nuts on my mind, Amy Jones.

"They're a good source of vitamin E. It'll help protect your liver, bring it up to speed while you keep your hands free of anything but water."

And there it is. Amy Jones caring for me, reaching out to me. Giving me a sign that she sees me, knows me. Is ready to be devoured by me.

Amy kept talking as she helped herself back in the car. "I'll bring you some after my shift! Or I'll tell Neil to deliver some to you."

Just like that, the butterflies collapsed to the floor of Richard's stomach. Neil. She'd send Neil over with the nuts that were on her mind. She waved from her car window, her fingers dancing wildly in the air, as she closed the door.

Richard sighed. Almonds. As if a few of Neil's nuts would turn his health around. He licked his cracked lips and cleared his scratchy throat. No; his body didn't want almonds. It didn't want Amy's nuts or Neil's nuts or anyone else's. It wanted a warm liquid to heat up his chest and make the eviction notice disappear from memory. Only three more days.

Just then as Amy drove off, her apartment door opened again. A dark-haired Neil walked out, looked to both sides of him, and crossed his arms as he gazed at the blinding sun.

If Neil Jones wanted to go blind, that was his decision. He was already blind to what he has...who he has, anyway. He had no idea the actual sunshine was within his possession.

Richard wanted to dart inside, find the fullest bottle of bourbon, and drink away the sight of Mr. Jones in front of him. He could do without that, as long as he could keep the Mrs. in his selective memory.

But before he was able to select which pieces to keep and which ones to drown away, the squeal of skidding wheels broke his attention. A noisy red car barrelled into the parking lot, halting to a skid when it found itself in Amy's parking space.

The hell is this?

Richard tried to sneak a look, see who was behind this recklessness, but from where he stood, his view of the driver was obscured. Whoever was in the driver's seat was no more than a shadow, an outline, and idea.

He watched Neil uncross his arms and broadened his smile. Then he became an old version of James Dean, leaning over the driver's side window, one hand propping himself up on the hood.

He stood like that for a minute. Maybe two. Then, Richard must have burned a hole that he felt. Neil stopped chatting with the mystery driver and met Richard's eyes. They felt like a judge's gavel. "How are you doing today, Richard? Did Amy tell you to get a walk out in this weather?"

Bang, bang. The gavel hit the desk. He saw right through Richard. He knew, didn't he? He knew his sight on Mrs. Jones was obvious. There might as well have been a neon sign over his head.

But Richard nodded. He answered the question. Yes; he did go for a walk. And, yes, Amy did tell him about the benefits of the weather. And, yes, Amy was the one who got to Richard first, making sure he was taken care of, that no one would have to worry about him.

"Good. She's right, you know. It's important to take care of yourself. The two of us aren't going to be here forever to give you these reminders."

That was the last thing Neil said before he hopped into the red car's passenger seat and sped away. The passenger's side door didn't even close before they took off.

And Neil was right. The Joneses wouldn't be there to watch over him forever. His mother was proof that forever wasn't promised.

If forever could be promised, he'd want to spend it in the sunshine.

But he couldn't. It wasn't meant for him.

So he found the cabinet above his refrigerator and opened it up to the lined bottles in a row.

"Suit up, boys."

CHAPTER SEVEN

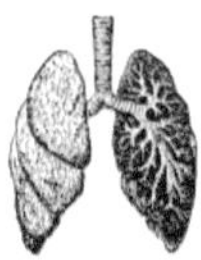

He pulled the pillowcase from its hiding place — in the small cabinet above the fridge, behind the bottles of alcohol normally lining themselves up — and watched the pattern of floral spikes slink between his fingers. The threadbare cotton fabric was faded from years of use and thousands of cycles through the wash.

Not his wash, though. He wanted to capture every scent, every breath, and every memory within the fibers of the fabric without ever washing them away. Washing it out would mean he'd be giving up everything he needed for himself. There was no way he'd let himself go back to choking on his own air. Going back wasn't an option.

Inhale. Drink in those scents. Feel their memories. Cough them out.

It was all still there, still promising him his collection.

But there was something wrong. When he opened it up to inspect the inside, it wasn't quite right. There was a rip, a tear, a cut. Not in the fabric. The fabric was fine, perfect, even. But in the customized plastic coating he took so long to place inside and tape together, making it a more precise tool. It was so easy to accumulate a load of those 'Have A Nice Day' plastic bags. It was almost like those yellow happy faces on them were happy to be put to good use. The little imperfection in one single face was making this a janky piece of crap. That wouldn't do.

He slipped it over his head and watched his surroundings darken. He took a deep breath in and choked on the absence of air. This, he was used to. This, he expected. But he also expected the covering to cling to him, hug his airways closed. He expected it to take effect immediately, not three seconds after engulfing him. It didn't. The hole inside had prevented it from doing its job. Exactly what he thought would happen.

He pulled it off his head, coughing his airways open. He'd have to fix that hole before his next outing. What was the point in going out at all if he wasn't completely prepared?

It wasn't the prettiest arts and crafts project, but it definitely got the job done. The tape stuck surprisingly well, and since he started using it, each job took a shorter amount of time than the last.

But if there was a hole, then there was a problem. It wouldn't be so quick. He'd have to suffer himself for longer while he struggled to take what was rightfully his. He didn't like that idea at all. He was suffering enough. There needed to be a fix that would do the job in a few swift seconds without a fight.

His annoyed fingers found the opening to the kitchen junk drawer — the land of spare screws, batteries, and odds and ends he stashed away from himself for later. He fished around inside until he found exactly what he needed: a roll of silver industrial tape.

The silverware drawer was next. Inside was a boning blade, the kind used to slice through chicken and steak bones with absurd ease. Like a hot knife through yellow fatty butter. Placing both the knife and the tape side by side on the counter, he picked up the pillowcase with the care of a fragile heirloom. It was well used, after all.

With a careful touch, he moved the pillowcase inside out and ran his hand over the rip. Thank goodness he saw this now instead of when he was night shopping next. That would have been a big headache and a major mistake. Noticing it now, during the day, out in the open of his empty home, was such a freaking relief.

He pulled a section of tape away from the roll and held it up. With his other hand, he sliced a section off. The boning knife did the trick. Just like butter. Impressive shivers crawled down his spine. This could make things more interesting, too.

One day, he would make sure to find out how interesting.

He flattened out the inside-out pillow case the best he could on the counter, with the plastic rip facing him. Ah, the offending spot. That'll get taken care of quickly. With the care of a surgeon, he placed the tape down and pressed it flat, sealing up the hole.

Ta-da. Done. Easy-peasy.

He admired his handiwork. There was no hole to be found, and now there was extra reinforcement. Pretty or not, this was the kind of arts and crafts project he was good at. One quick slab of tape and it was ready to go.

He pulled the pillowcase right side out again. The little sprigs of blue lavender were now bumpy with the extra tape. Both hands pressed down, attempting to smooth it out, but it still rippled underneath. He frowned. It wasn't perfect. But some people liked a little extra texture. He took it as a win.

He lifted the corners up and felt the weight pull up from the counter and dangle momentarily in the air. A wandering curiosity crept through his mind.

Did I fix it well enough? Is it going to work the way I want?

He slipped it back over his head, making sure it covered everything — his nose, his mouth, every hole possible.

He inhaled as much as he could. Like magic, his masterpiece clung to his mouth and nose, preventing any extra air from going in or out. A shot of adrenaline rippled through him before he let out a series of suffocated coughs.

It had worked. It had really worked. It was fixed, which made it as perfect as it could be, even with the extra bumps.

This was the only time where he was thankful he couldn't breathe.

He slipped the cloth up, away from his airways, and he could inhale again. Not comfortably. He could never actually breathe comfortably, but he could breathe. Comfort would come later. It would come with his excitement. This was just a taste of the next fresh breath he could take, and that was good enough for now.

Letting the pillowcase rest on his head like a nightcap, he picked up the roll of duct tape and slid it back into the junk drawer.

Goodbye, friend.

The boning knife was now left alone on the counter. The blade's curvature smiled back at him. He gave it a twisted grin, too.

You, my friend, you'll be used one day. Just be patient.

He picked up the handle and marveled at how reflective the metal was. It was such a pretty thing, like a painted woman with curves that could make his heart pitter-patter.

"Lavender's blue, diddle diddle." The song started to creep from his lips. "Lavender's green."

"Amelia Jones! How are ya?"

His eyes shot wide open and agitated butterflies crisscrossed in his stomach.

What was *she* doing here? And why was Gladys Nightingale always so freaking loud about *her* arrival?

Maybe this was good. He should thank her.

Thank you, Gladys.

He ripped the pillowcase off his head and shoved it haphazardly back in the cabinet above his refrigerator. His cabinet of secrets. Sweat poured out of him, tucking in the corners away from sight.

He slammed the door shut.

Done. Gone. Safely away.

He ran into the living room to quickly look out the front window. Movement on the front porch reminded him that there was something still in his hand.

Crap. The blade.

The doorknob jiggled, twisting and turning from the other side.

The freaking boning blade!

He opened a drawer on the tiny table next to the couch and slid the knife inside.

Gone. It was gone and out of sight.

"Got any news to share?" Gladys's rough voice begged.

And did he have to move so quickly? That old woman was taking her sweet time.

"Glad you asked, Gladys! I'm going to a health conference in a couple of days."

A couple of days. He only had a couple of days. That was it.

"I'm going to see if I can bring home some trial patches or something for you to test out. See if we can help you put down the smoking habit."

Her voice, smooth like butter, woke up the butterflies inside of him. They looped-the-loop and he couldn't control the perspiration from pouring out of his forehead.

He opened the front door and was greeted by a head of blonde curls.

"Hi, Amy."

Her.

CHAPTER EIGHT

The school parking lot shot Richard back at least twenty-three years. As a thirty-two-year-old man, he was in the car, his mother behind the wheel. Except, he wasn't thirty-two; he was nine years old. And he was cradling his backpack on his lap, answering questions that should have been asked before they ever left out the front door.

"Is your homework in your backpack?"
"Yes, Mom."
"And your form for the science project?"
"It's in there, too."
"And you have socks on under those shoes, right?"
"Of course."
"How about—"
"No, Mom. I left my dime at home."
"Keep your most precious things in the safest of places and you'll always have them close to heart."

Richard's special dime. He had been told it was too valuable to stuff in his jeans pocket and tote around school. He believed it, too.

But one day, he ignored the warning and brought it to school to show the other kids. Patty Parker asked to look at it after he told the group of students around him what his mother said about it being so special. She plucked it from his hand and tossed it to the third row of seats.

He heard it *ping* on the tile then roll away to land somewhere between the chasm of chair and table legs.

"That's just a stupid dime," Patty Parker scoffed.

And that was when Richard looked at the gangly girl with chestnut hair and decided *she* wasn't special. With pin straight hair and a plain face that wore the kind of expression that said, "I know way more than anyone else," she was just an ordinary girl who didn't know anything at all. There was nothing extraordinary about someone who couldn't see what was right in front of them.

That was the day he had scrambled like a spider across the floor on hands and knees to find his dime. When he had finally found it in the shadow of Gregory Jorge's backpack, he pinched it between two tentative fingers and slipped it back into his pocket, never to see school grounds again.

And now, here Richard was, facing the same elementary school where Patty Parker proved she was too dull to shine. Only, standing in the winding bus loop wasn't Patty Parker.

It was Amy Jones.

The sky was open and the rays were wide. Amy Jones was here.

The sour schoolboy memory faded the moment Richard saw her unload a box full of dried pasta out of the back of a grocery truck. Only Amy could make lifting a box of boxes look sexy. Her back arched. Her hips swung. Her hands gripped the sides of the box tight, strong. But of course Amy could make it look hot. She was the sun. Everything she did was hot.

To be that box, feel that grip…

Even the way she lifted boxes of pasta out and onto a table made him want to run to her, wrap his arms around her midsection, and pull her skin against his. He wanted to smell the soap on her. He wanted to feel how soft her cheek was. He wanted the flutter of her eyelashes to tickle his nose in butterfly kisses.

Richard's butterflies tickled each other in their own kisses.

He wanted her in all the ways he knew he couldn't.

There was a knock on his window.

Dave?

No, not Good Ol' Dave. A man with a painted smile stood outside his window. His finger pointed toward the pavement, begging Richard to roll it down for him.

So he did. He rolled it down, and the painted smile dropped into a frown. "Oh," he wiggled his nose as the air from inside Richard's truck drifted out into the open. "If you're here to pick up, you can go ahead and pull into the bus loop. We'll load everything up for you within a few minutes." He tried to bring the smile back, but the pained expression broke the effort.

His truck didn't smell *that* bad, did it?

A sniff. A whiff. It didn't smell bad at all. It smelled like an invitation to open a fresh bottle right then and there.

He declined the invitation. Amy wouldn't approve. Not during a volunteer event she begged him to be at.

"No, I'm not here for pick up." Richard shook his head. "I'm here to volunteer."

"Oh." The painted smile strained itself back into place. "Well, we could absolutely use the help. It's only me and Amelia today, and we're expecting several pickups within the next few hours."

"Amy." The correction slipped out of Richard's mouth. The butterflies pushed it out before he could think twice about it.

"Oh, good, you already know her. No need for introductions. We can get started right away. Come on, now. Let's see where we can put you to work."

Richard followed the man's lead to the sidewalk in the front of the building. Five folding tables lined up under the shade of tents. Each one held a stack of brown bags ready to be opened and filled with the assortment of cans and boxes scattered on the table. Green beans. Corn. Microwavable meals. Canned meat. Dry noodles in every type and fashion.

Spaghetti sauce.

"Richard! You're here!" Amy's voice melted from the back of the delivery truck. She had another large box in her hand, and even though her smile beamed right at him, he could see her arms shaking with the weight inside of it.

It was heavy. Much too heavy for Amy's frame.

And this was Richard's chance.

Instinctively, Richard slid his hands under the box. For a split second, his thumbs brushed against her pinkies. It was just a second, but it was the entire world, his entire timeline. The touch woke up the butterflies in his stomach, making them loop the loop in slow motion tangled circles.

"Oh my goodness, thank you so much!" Amy was so close. He really could smell the soap on her skin. And her breath. It was like sweetened vanilla.

"You're welcome," his breath answered back. And even though he knew his own smell was sour next to hers, she didn't flinch. Her smile still beamed.

She's accepting me as is.

He had to order the butterflies to cease their motion, to calm down. This wasn't his sunshine to be had, and he knew it. He was only here to help serve his community. That was it, right? There was no other reason for him to be standing here, face to face with Samhale's sweetheart, sweating from his armpits, and attempting to keep his thirst at bay.

Down, butterflies.

"Over there," Amy pointed her finger to the closest table. "Just empty out what's inside so we can sort everything into the bags for the families who come to pick up."

Richard nodded. He wanted to salute her or bow or do something to show he was ready to take her orders. If only there she could give them out to him like specialized candy. Do this, do that.

Yes, ma'am!

But eagerness wasn't within him. It couldn't be. No one is eager to absorb the sun, it just happens. You walk outside and it's there. Same with Amy. She just radiated, naturally.

He obeyed his one order and robotically reached in the box to pull out the contents one by one.

Jars of pineapple and peaches clinked together next to a large glass container of applesauce. He placed each on the table in a pile of the world's saddest fruit cocktail. Yet, it still looked more appealing than anything in his own kitchen.

"Make sure you organize them into piles. It'll help us sort them out evenly to everyone who shows up." The butterflies in Richard's stomach might as well have been nonexistent. Poof. Painted Smile's voice killed their craving for flight.

"Got it," Richard mumbled back.

So he went to work organizing. He placed all the new jars of fruit together, then stacked the canned vegetables in a row. Canned meats came next as well as rice, couscous, and other grains.

Richard didn't even know what couscous was, but he imagined Amy did.

It sounded organic and healthy, and something that was probably a staple item in the Joneses' pantry, where Amy would put it to use in fancy meals…

The butterflies fluttered alive again.

…with her husband at the dinner table on Wednesday nights.

And just like that, they quieted their wings.

Richard imagined himself in Neil's seat, scooping a bite of couscous onto his fork and lifting it to his mouth, watching Amy do the same. He thought about how that fork would enter her mouth, slowly, teasingly, coating her tongue with the flavors of… butter? Corn? Cream? Salt? Whatever couscous was supposed to taste like mixed with the sweetness of *her*. He imagined her closing her eyes, enjoying every little grain as it rolled across her tongue and slid down her throat.

Flip. Flap.

His mouth was so dry.

"Lookin' good, Richard!" Amy's voice echoed to him as she carried another box from the truck to the second table and unloaded it.

How amazing was she to carry one just as heavy without complaining or asking for help? She just did it.

"If you don't mind, could you help unload more of these before the driver has to leave?"

And how amazing was she to ask for help when she needed it?

She nodded her head to the box in her hands. "There are just a few more left in the truck."

And how amazing was she to take care of her load while asking for someone else to take care of theirs?

But Richard wasn't here to list off all the reasons why Amy Jones was so spectacular. He wasn't there to watch her ass sway while she carried boxes back and forth. And he wasn't there to daydream about stepping into her husband's shoes and scoop up all the sunshine that would have belonged to him.

As Richard made his way back and forth from the truck to the tables, he gave himself a mantra to remember why he was there. The real reason why he should be there. "For the community. For the good. For the sunshine." He had promised Amy he would do better. Today, he was going to prove it. Today, he would actually do something to make her proud. Maybe he would even make her look at him the way he hoped he wasn't outwardly looking at her.

But every time he thought of the last part of his mantra, he pictured touching Amy's blonde locks and imagined how they'd fit between his fingers. Then, his hands would sweat and his butterflies would wrap themselves tightly in his chest and he'd have to start the mantra over again.

"All right, team, looks like our first car is here!" Painted Smile beamed his energy toward Richard.

A van with chipping tan paint pulled into the school parking lot, rolling on brakes that sounded like they weren't going to actually brake. Richard watched Painted Smile greet the driver and ask how many people were in the home.

Easy enough.

"Six," the man behind the wheel said.

Okay, it still seemed simple.

With the single word, Amy joined Painted Smile in a well rehearsed dance Richard never learned the steps to. Together, they filled up three boxes, tossing in enough food to feed an army of a dozen people for at least a week. Amy passed the box to Painted Smile and he filed in the boxes to the back of the van she opened for him. They closed the door together, tapped on the side of the car…

Tap tap tap

… and waved goodbye with a, "Thank you," from the driver.

The entire number lasted less than thirty seconds. This was more complicated. And Richard was never very good at learning dance numbers. He wasn't much of a lead.

Next was a yellow sedan. Richard was ready. He was going to take the lead, show he had the skills. But the moment he picked up a box, he missed his cue. "Four." And the well rehearsed couple was already packed up and *tap tap tapping* on the side of the car.

Same thing happened with a blue SUV. Even though he already packed in a box to the brim, readying himself, the two of them glided over and filled up the car. By the time they waved goodbye, Richard had just enough time to stumble, trip, and dump out all the contents of the box he had been holding all over the sidewalk.

A white car with a green passenger's door also pulled up on shaky wheels. And again, Amy and the Painted Smile man moved in step with each other without a single flaw. Pack in the boxes. Load the car. Smile and wave.

It wasn't fair. Painted Smile wasn't even her husband. He didn't deserve to bask in the Amy-shine. He didn't put on a ring and make vows and decide to care for her forever and ever.

Not that Richard had, either. But *he* didn't overstep his boundaries. He made sure of that. He knew his place in her world. He was her neighbor. He could be a sad charity case if he allowed her to acknowledge it. But he wasn't. He was a neighbor. A kind neighbor.

A kind neighbor who dreamt of her sleeping next to him at night, curling up to her curves, learning the way she danced between the sheets, consuming every ounce of her she would allow.

But that was it. End of story.

The butterflies within him forced their wings to settle as he picked up the spilled items on the sidewalk. He swore under his breath, knowing that his presence was slowing down a system that shouldn't have this weird, permanently smiling man in it.

And then the scream of an angry engine tore through the parking lot, forcing its way to the front of the bus loop line.

That was when Amy's emerald eyes shot bullets Richard didn't know they carried. Her eyes furrowed and her voice grew deadpan, "I'll take care of this one." Amy wrapped her arms around the box Richard was holding. Her mouth said, "Thank you," but her eyes read fear.

The box wasn't even full. There were still scattered supplies scattered everywhere.

The butterflies did loops. He knew that feeling well. He had carried fear for months, letting its cold persistence pump through his veins. He had been struggling to dull the chill with every bottle he picked up. And yet, here was Amy keeping her composure as she reached the car's open window and fit the box through it like an ill-fitting puzzle piece. For a moment, looking at her standing next to this vehicle, he could see Neil's silhouette leaning against the door, his smile charming his way into the ease of conversation.

It was the same damned red car.

"Hey, Richard, could you help me out over here?" Painted Smile broke his attention, pointing to the line forming. Each car had another tired driver waiting for a set of predetermined groceries chosen just for them and the number they gave.

Clumsily, Richard mimicked Painted Smile's movements. He picked up a box or a bag. He filled it up. And he clumsily helped fill the cars.

Only he *tapped* when he should have *tap tap tapped*.

And he couldn't figure out how to close the trunks without slamming them.

And even though he waved goodbye, it also felt like a wave of "Sorry" rather than "Thank you."

Painted Smile wasn't impressed. His facial expressions looked even more fake than ever.

One by one, they filled the cars, waving each driver along, telling them to pass the red car stopped in front.

That red car. There was something special about it. Not in a drunken loop-the-loop butterfly way, but in an emerald fire way. Whoever was behind the wheel of that car had fired up Amy, and that made Richard's insides boil.

"Richard! Over here!" Painted Smile waved him over to a dirt-covered Jeep. So, he filled another box and dragged it over, less quickly than either of his cohorts would have done on their own.

He felt the fire of Amy's eyes dig into him, scratching its way under his skin and squeezing his chest tighter than before. The look she gave was masked with composure, but he was sure that there was something tearing at her beneath the surface.

"One more box, Richard." If Painted Smile could arch his expression any more, he would look like a deranged clown without makeup.

He *was* a deranged clown without makeup.

With a huff, Richard grabbed another box and fed it through another car door. If he could bring his mind to focus, then he was sure he'd be able to narrow these step-by step moves a little easier. Though dancing with this deranged man was nothing like what he imagined it would be dancing with *her*.

When the last blue CRV drove off, Richard's eyes found themselves watching the curve of the bus loop. The red car was gone, but Amy was still there. Still, like a statue with shallow breath.

"You okay, Amy?" Painted Smile called from behind Richard's back. "You all right?"

She nodded her head. Sunshine poured from her smile, but the warm rays never reached her eyes. Or Richard. And he felt sad about that.

"Of course I'm okay," she called back. But her gaze didn't leave from where the red car last stood. "How many more do we have?"

Richard looked behind him. None. They had serviced all the cars.

Good job, Richard.

All the drivers and their numbers had their packages of pantry supplies in hand. But before he could answer her, Richard saw Painted Smile's face drop. Within a flash, he was gone from sight, rushing his way to Amy.

The butterflies' wings drooped and what he saw in front of him tore himself in two. Painted Smile's arms were wrapped around Amy.

That should have been his arms.

Her green eyes closed so tight, hiding their golden flecks from the world.

He should have held her.

Painted Smile's hand stroked her golden curls, losing his fingers within the rowdy tendrils.

Those curls were part of Richard's fantasy.

A vise wrapped around Richard's chest, squeezing his lungs closed and the butterflies still. He pulled his hands to his face and examined every inch. Every finger that once held yellowed curls. Every knuckle that danced within blonde hair. Every inch of his palm that wore sticky red sauce he couldn't wash away from memory.

He wanted to run over to her. He wanted to pull Painted Smile off her body and watch her face turn into something more manageable, more normal. He wanted to wrap his own arms around Amelia Jones, pull her close to him and breathe her in. Whatever just happened to her broke the sunshine within her and he couldn't take it.

This wasn't his place. Holding her wasn't his job. He hadn't even learned the dance.

A snapping noise rapped in his head.

This wasn't for him.

She wasn't for him.

Before either of the other two had the time to notice, Richard's feet moved. They pounded the pavement as he clutched his heart all the way back to his truck.

She wasn't for him. *Not yet.*

But those soldiers were. He'd welcome their darkness.

CHAPTER NINE

A sharp intake of air hit Richard's lungs, and his eyes darted out of the darkness. This felt wrong. Real wrong.

There was no living room carpet under him. His feet weren't dangling off his bed.

He didn't even feel the metal insides of a Kwick-Mart shopping cart.

His back hurt. His eyes burned. The smell of trash made the butterflies run for cover.

Outside. Crap.

He wasn't home.

He sat upright, trying to make sense of where he was waking up now.

Bang.

His head hit something hard, ringing everything from his ears to the pit of his stomach. And now his head hurt, too.

Alright, Richard, figure out where the hell you are.

The chatty buzz of flies circled around a large dumpster. But the smell seeping into him was worse than trash: A metal canister filled with plastic bags and dog crap. Familiar dog barks rang his ears even more.

He was home. Just not at his home.

He was in the grassy knoll behind the apartment complex where residents tossed their trash and local teens hid away to taste their first sips of booze.

This was where Amy once held a barbeque in an attempt to draw out connections between neighbors who would rather keep to themselves. He could picture it now. Amy reaching into a cooler for a bottle of water, condensation dripping down her arm. Watching her cool herself with the same dripping water on the side of her cheek, down her neck, and sneaking itself down the front of her shirt. Feeling the tips of her fingers brush against his while accepting a sprig of lavender as a gift. Tucking that same sprig behind her ears and wanting to taste her lobes to see if they were as sweet as the lavender smelled.

But that was ages ago. And now he was here, alone, sitting on his back steps where the dog poo was stinking up a storm.

He stretched and looked around. Wrong again; he wasn't by his back door. He was sitting on the bottom step two doors down. He was right outside the back door of number 76, the Joneses' apartment.

Richard used the handrail he bumped his head on to ease himself to a stand. At least he was in the back. No one getting in and out of the parking lot would see him take a walk of shame two doors down.

He rubbed his eyes with a forefinger and thumb, trying to drone out a headache that was bound to brew. But even with his eyes closed, he felt strands of hair between his fingers coated in red sauce and sadness. He squeezed his fists tight, wondering why he hadn't been able to drown out the nightmares yet.

After all this time, he still felt his mother's hair in his hands. The blonde curls he always loved. Hair just like…

He forced his eyes open to the daylight. To the sunshine.

To Amy.

He turned to face the back door at the top of the steps. This was where the kitchen would be. Behind the frosted window pane, Amy Jones would pace in the kitchen, cooking up lentils and vegetables, and couscous and whatever else healthy people — good people — ate.

This was where she would store her boxes of oranges and canisters of almonds, just waiting for the chance to be donated to a sad, needy individual like Richard.

This was where her husband would join her and place his hands around her waist, swaying to the music on the radio while she chopped carrots and onions for a dinner salad.

Richard hugged his arms around himself at the thought, pretending a pretty blonde was in front of him. Feeling his hands around her waist, swaying his body as if she were swaying hers against his.

A form appeared behind the glass pane. The opaque frost made it difficult for Richard to see who it was, but he could make out the outline of a tiny waist and a curvy rear end. This had to be Amy. This had to be the sunshine he had to focus on to drown out all the darkness that was creeping up on him.

She moved toward the refrigerator. She opened the door, and Richard could see the outline of her rounded curves as she bent over and danced on the balls of her feet. Whatever she was contemplating on removing from the fridge was being teased as much as he was.

Another shadow entered the kitchen. Taller than the first with broad shoulders and a messy outline of hair. Neil Jones. He threw a hand back and hit the rounded rear end of the curvy figure bending over.

There was a brief yelp and he could hear the fridge door slam shut. The two figures morphed into one shadow full of fits of giggles and squeals. An arm reached up and touched the top of the taller person's head.

Richard touched his own hair and ruffled the dusky tendrils between his fingers. His hair could be messy, and moppy, too.

The taller form bent down and wrapped its two arms around the smaller shadow, picking it up with the ease of a single movement.

Richard wrapped his arms around himself again, bent his knees, then straightened up, hugging himself harder. He could lift her up just as easily and feel her weight ground him into happiness.

The two people spun together in a circle, the giggling fits growing louder, teasing Richard's ears.

Richard closed his eyes and spun in a circle, too. He let the giggling fill him up, telling himself he could create that sound, too. But the topmost step proved not enough space. He twirled right off it and tumbled to the bottom. Concrete corners jabbed into his ankles and grass stained the bottom of his jeans when he skidded to a stop on the ground.

Richard rolled both ankles in a circle to assess the damage. They hurt, but they moved fine enough. He would probably have to be careful, take it easy. No sudden movements.

With both palms on the ground, Richard lifted himself up to a stand. He needed another dose of vitamin D to make him forget what just happened. But when he looked through the frosted pane, it was empty. There were no shadowy figures standing or dancing or giggling in number 76's kitchen.

Where did they go?

Curiosity got the best of him.

If he couldn't have a vantage point from the back view, he'd try the front.

Walking carefully, Richard crept his way away from the Joneses' apartment and toward the corner unit. No, not crept. He snuck.

The corner unit was the only one with an extra window, and when he passed it, the dogs sounded off their calls again. Louder this time, alerting the entire complex there was something they wanted to get at on the other side of the window.

Shut up, dogs!

The parking lot welcomed him with a car in every other parking spot in front of the matching yellow doors. And right in front of number 76 was the same freaking red car as before. The one Neil leaned against so nonchalantly and the one that made Amy Jones cry at the food pantry.

His butterflies wrapped around his lungs and squeezed.

So hard to breathe.

He moved past the car and went straight for the steps. He allowed his feet to land on the first step, then the second. By the time he reached the top, he was second-guessing what he was doing at the Joneses' front door.

Amy Jones wasn't his. She was promised to Neil.

But it wouldn't hurt to look, right? Looking didn't hurt anyone.

Unlike the back door, the front had no window pane, just a single peephole for residents to look out. But there was one large window to the left of the door, which gave an even bigger view. On the other side of it was the living room. It really wouldn't hurt to peek in. It would be no different than looking in from a parking space. Just a little closer, with a better view.

Richard leaned himself over the handrail. The window's curtain obstructed his view a little, but it was sheer. If he squinted, maybe he could see where they went.

He squinted. He didn't see.

But there was a squeal again, so he gave it another minute. He imagined the sound came from one of the rooms with a closed door. Maybe he pinched her ass. Not hard, just a little play. Everyone liked a little play … even a little pain. He reached a hand behind himself and grabbed his own ass cheek and gave it a little pinch.

"Whatcha doin', Richard Teft?"

Gladys's voice sent him straight into the air. She must have gotten bored of her daily soap opera, and decided to venture outside in search of some other excitement.

And the excitement she caught was him. Looking into Amy's window, pinching his own ass cheek.

"Nothing, Gladys. Just…" He gave another look at the door, trying to come up with an explanation. "I wasn't doing anything."

Gladys's eyes bore into him, begging for something to fill her curiosity.

"I guess I just got a little lost."

She chuffed. "Yeah, I bet. You just got lost in Amelia, huh?"

The butterflies felt queasy, sick, thirsty.

"I didn't say that, Gladys." Richard made his way down the steps and over to his own apartment, leaving the sunshine behind him. "I just got a little sidetracked on where I was going. That's all."

"I'd say you got sidetracked." Gladys blew out a string of smoke and watched it climb the air.

He shook his head. "If there was anything going on, you'd know about it before anyone else."

Which stood to make sense. Nosey old ladies would know more than anyone else if they tried hard enough.

But, before Gladys could provoke him any further, he turned open his doorknob. Thank goodness he had left it unlocked for himself. He couldn't imagine what he would look like trying to climb through a window to get back inside.

As he let himself into his apartment, the silhouetted figures plagued his memory. Two figures dancing together, laughing, shrieking.

The frosted glass obscured the images into shadows and it made him feel more alone than ever. Two could play that game.

The open cabinet smiled at Richard's washed gaze. Waiting for him was a row of disheveled bottles. Bourbon, brandy, and vodka. All the little off-duty soldiers lazily waiting to be called to war.

Vodka was up. It wasn't his drink of choice, but his taste buds couldn't afford to be picky.

While he waited for the first gulp to bring him back to blackness, he pulled out his phone and mindlessly scrolled through social media.

He stopped at Amy's photo, clicked on her smile, and came face to face with her latest post.

A shared event. A two-day retreat for health nuts and exercise buffs. Amy would fit right in there and from the looks of it, she was planning on going. At least, that was what the exclamation points in her comment to the event made Richard believe.

Underneath was a photo of her and Neil with ear-to-ear grins standing outside the Samhale Library. Next to the Joneses was a third person. Richard recognized her as one of the regular librarians from the many times he had popped in for an air-conditioned break while working on a project he was hired to do by the county. With grayed eyes and a wide-set nose, she shared nothing of Amy except … her hair.

Curly, blonde hair.

Richard gulped down another swig and read the caption. "I can't believe we lost Leslie, Samhale's most amazing and knowledgeable librarian. I'm so glad I got to spend many volunteer hours with you. RIP, Leslie Arlene. May they find who did this to you and bring you justice."

CHAPTER TEN

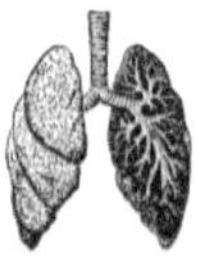

The earth under his feet felt alive, like a little heartbeat that awoke beneath him. It lifted him up off the ground, springing him into tiptoed steps. The movement fed into his excitement even more. He pulled his leather gloves over his hands as he inched his way through the dark of night. He was thankful he had thought ahead to keep them close by, just in case he needed them.

There was no 'just in case'. He knew he would need them.

The house's side window gave him the perfect view. Positioned behind a living room couch, he could see the outline of her light hair. Her unruly locks twisted and turned, agitated from a long day. She was still on the couch, unmoving, probably reading a book, unsuspecting of his eyes soaking in her image.

"Lavender blue...diddle diddle."

She shifted to another position and craned her neck to adjust its tension.

Ha. Tension. He pulled on the front of his jeans to relieve his.

His back pocket *dinged,* and he silently cursed to himself. How could he have been so forgetful? He should have turned the sound off his cell phone earlier, before he made his way down this street, up this driveway, and outside this window.

Idiot.

He choked out a sigh. The window wasn't open yet. No one else heard the ding. No one else cared. He was all by himself with a tiny hiccup in his duty.

Got lucky, that time.

A hand reached to his back pocket and slipped the phone out. His brows furrowed when he read what was there:

A: **I'm ready to play when you are.**

No; he wasn't ready to play. Not now. Now wasn't the time for games. Now was the time for work. Not the stupid work everyone else in Samhale thought was necessary at their survival jobs to pay bills. Not even the kind of work that was disguised as volunteering with the kindness of your heart. It was the kind of work that was actually necessary. It was the kind of work that would set him free.

And once he was free, he could play as recklessly as he wanted.

His thumb hit the mute button and slipped the phone back into his pocket, where it would wait until later. He gazed back up through the window and saw her again.

She may not have known him well, but he knew her. And all the others like her. She volunteered at the weekly food drive, serving hungry people in their community. She gave out smiles just as freely as the food itself. He had no doubt she felt like she was a better person because of it.

She kept deceptive control over the people who couldn't afford their own meals. She reveled in the fact that she was a protector, feeding them when they couldn't fulfill their own necessity. Had she not filled the shoes of a protector, all of these people would suffer. The thought suffocated him, and he needed to breathe.

A scratchy feeling ran down his throat and through his lungs.

He rolled his back to the house's siding and slid his way to a crouch above the freshly manicured grass. Gloves on, he checked his shoe strings. Tight. Secure. He zipped his black hoodie. Snug. Shielding.

"I heard one say, diddle diddle."

He glanced up at the large oak tree nearby and scoffed. A childhood dream died there long ago. Had he known what shape that dream would form later in life, he would have never spent those hours in the branches, dangling in laughter with *her*. He wouldn't have shared his dreams or carved them into the raised roots with *her*.

That tree meant so much and so little to him. It held everything that brought him to this point, here, now. And it was also where his dreams died. Freedom wasn't a natural part of his life now. So he made sure he showed up to claim freedom where he could. Until he could have *her*.

Turning his back on the tree, he faced the window again. She had adjusted herself to the corner of the couch, her posture indicating sleep was creeping up. He imagined the book she had been reading was probably sliding down to a resting point. Her head was probably drifting off to the side. Her body was probably relaxing into suspended consciousness.

It was almost time.

His fingers pressed against the window, and he forced them to move up. As he expected, the window cracked open with a slight hiss to allow in the open air.

Good. Diddle diddle.

At the hissing sound, he reflexively moved away from the glass pane. Heart pounding with excitement, he was sure she had heard it too. He had never started his tasks with someone so close to his entry before. He had no idea how a young and awake target would react. The added obstacle escalated the thrill.

He adjusted his pants again.

Mentally, he counted to ten. Each number was deliberate and slow, helping to collect his thoughts and regulate his heartbeat.

One.

He closed his eyes and pictured his suffocation lifting. The pressure easing from his lungs and throat.

Two.

Every inch toward releasing the hold she had on him was an inch closer to his own free breaths. And even though he couldn't have *her* — not yet — he was closer to providing his own release. And that was enough for now, at least.

Three.

Each time he hit his mark, his lungs opened up a little more. Each time was another breath of fresh air, another step closer to opening his airways completely.

Four.

But this time, he was sure he'd be closer to the freedom he wanted. One step closer to having *her*.

Five.

Had enough time passed? Would she have turned her back away from his view?

Six. Seven. Eight.

Maybe it would be better to keep counting, give her time to settle back into her self-serving stance.

No. Nine.

He inhaled, telling himself his shallow breaths would be able to deepen soon. He stifled a cough as the air caught in his lungs. He wanted to climb in, be there next to her. Feel the air seep out of her lungs so he could fill his own. He controlled his breath out, fighting back his eagerness. It would happen in time. He didn't have to rush.

Opening his eyes, he took his stance by the window again. There she was, back in the corner of the couch, book in hand, soaking in her parasitic selflessness.

He pushed his gloved hands over the window again and slid them up to give himself more room. It moved without a sound, just the way he liked it. The house breathed in the fresh air outside, and he felt a twinge of jealousy of how easily it did.

With lungs as full as they would allow, he held his breath. His arms and legs moved as soundlessly as the window did, hoisting himself up to the ledge. He swiveled his knees inward and dropped his feet to the floor. The couch was a foot away from his reach and his heart fluttered a beat when she moved her hand to tuck a stray blonde strand behind her ear.

He could smell the flowers from the other room. They must have been well taken care of, snipped fresh from the garden. But he wanted to be able to inhale even deeper, take in the fragrances as if they were right next to him.

Stealthily, he reached into his hoodie pocket and slipped out his stowed away pillowcase. Fixed. Mended. Ready for action.

He opened it up with ease. Thanks to a side table lamp, he could see inside the opening. How ironic to see the limited air space inside.

Exhaling the air he had been keeping hostage, he allowed a single word to slip out, "Ten."

There wasn't enough time to read the expression on her face. He had slipped the pillowcase over her head too quickly for that. As he gathered the edges of fabric around her neck, she scrambled her arms to free herself. He could feel her body moving toward him, and he silently thanked himself again for being so smart to line it with plastic.

"Lavender's green," he hissed, and pressed her shoulders down. "Diddle diddle."

Now pinning her between himself and the couch, he reached into his pocket again. He was eager to put a new tool to work. He had promised its curved-blade smile that he would test it out, see what it could do. And now he was curious. He breathed in deeply, already feeling his lung capacity growing.

The pointed tip hovered over her chest, tracing little circles over where her heart was. The kind of heart that was open for all the people in Samhale, ready to do whatever it was they needed. The kind of heart that fed off the goodness she forced onto the community.

She jolted her body back and forth. It twisted this way and that like a convulsing snake trying to wriggle its way free. Her muffled yelps shallowed with every movement. Somehow, one hand escaped from his grasp and jolted into the air. He wasn't concerned, though. It wouldn't take much longer now. He watched with curiosity as the fingers opened and closed, searching for something to grasp onto or push off

He could do that. With his free hand, he linked his fingers with hers. It felt so foreign and held none of the warmth he had expected. It was like holding onto a plastic mannequin. Cold. Smooth, and semi-artificial. The hand didn't even clasp back like a human hand should. Especially from a person who was supposed to hold onto community members and guide them into something better than what they had.

That stupid hand. He hated it. But it was also proof that his actions were justifiable. All these do-gooders were only in it for themselves. So if he had to take their breaths for himself, then so be it. There wasn't an inch of guilt that ran through his veins.

While lacing his fingers with the hand in front of him, he lifted his blade again. When the tip of it touched the back of the hand, the fingers extended out like a tense spider readying its legs.

But when the blade entered the skin, the little spider in his gloved hand shriveled in front of him. It was a little boring watching it go limp so suddenly, so he dragged the knife up the wrist and forearm, drawing a neat little line he could watch bleed

The warm liquid that poured out was far more fascinating to watch. It made little spiderwebs that climbed toward her elbow, and when he finally let go of the fingers, the spider webs crawled onto the floor, staining the carpet in dark puddles.

He kept watching in fascination, waiting for the moment when the red river would dry up. Eventually, it had stopped, and he pulled back to admire the abstract artwork he left behind. He took in a delicious, deep breath. This was so much better than it had been before. He was so much closer to breaking out of his suffocation indefinitely.

The only problem was, he knew breathing again would only last a short while with this one. The suffocation always came back, and he'd have to open his airways again. There was only one way he could clear them out for good.

All it would take was one more task. One more breath to claim.

And it would be *hers*.

He'd have to take Amy Jones's last breath to free himself completely.

CHAPTER ELEVEN

A bead of sweat dripped from Richard's eyebrow and landed on the pavement. He watched a tiny dark circle form at his feet. How he felt so hot was beyond him. The weather wasn't oppressive. The blooming wind should have kept him cool. The sun wasn't anywhere close to full blast.

The sun.

Richard sucked in a deep breath. He could use the sun. Not the one in the sky, but the one that lived two doors down. He drank in another breath and felt the air scratch at his insides. He needed a dose of his sunshine. Well, not his. But he was sure he could still take an innocent peek without anyone, including Neil, caring very much.

His feet did the walking without his brain doing much thinking. He would just get a little peek, that's it. See what he could see. Fill himself up with the sunshine from a distance and walk back home. That was it.

The front window was the easiest access. No one would have suspected anything if he was walking up to the front door. He could just tell Gladys or the corner unit dog owners that he was checking in on a neighbor. That was a thing normal people did. Wasn't it?

Another step toward door number 76 and Richard's throat went dry. He promised himself he would fix that later. He'd take in one addiction before he would feed himself another. That seemed like the healthy thing to do.

Another step and Richard's breath hitched in his throat. A deep bark cut through his thoughts and a flash of black fur darted straight toward him. One of the dogs in the corner unit was barreling down the sidewalk at top speed, tongue lapping out of his mouth and lips pulled back to show his teeth.

The damned dog was going to attack him.

"Duke!" Richard never bothered to learn the names of either of the people who lived in the corner unit, and if he had ever heard the dogs' names, he definitely didn't remember them. But he was pretty sure Duke was the dog, because it was a man yelling his name. "Duke!" The normally quiet man from the corner unit was running in top speed right behind the dog.

The last thing Richard saw were the points of Duke's white teeth, dripping with drool and right in front of his face.

The black lab jumped from its stance, landing its two front paws on Richard's chest. Both of them fell to the pavement together and a pain shot from around Richard's back and up his side.

"Get off me, dog!"

"Duke!"

Richard could hear the man from the corner unit, but he couldn't see past the heavy breathing dog on his chest.

"Off, dog!" He pushed his palms on the dog's chest and tried to move the beast off him. But every time he pushed with his hands, the dog pushed back, moving forward, tongue lapping at the air in front of his face.

The sour saliva dripped from the bottom of Duke's mouth and onto Richard's cheek. It smeared across his mouth and dangled on his bottom lip. He wanted to wipe the viscous fluid away. He had things to do, sunshine to absorb, and this mutt had to go and ruin it for him. It took everything in Richard to keep his hands in place, pressing against the dog's chest to keep both him and the dog from attacking each other any further.

"Duke!" The man sounded close now, right on top of Duke himself. Sure enough, Richard felt the weight of the dog lift off his chest and the gamey smell of its breath lessen.

With the weight of the dog off him completely, Richard sat up straight on the ground. He was now eye to eye with his attacker, the typically quiet man holding him back by the collar.

"I am so sorry! We were about to go for a walk, and he just bolted out the front door. That never happens."

At the sound of the word *walk*, Duke barked and pulled from his owner's grip. The man's arm jolted forward, but he held him back from getting away.

"He's such a lovey boy, isn't he?"

"Lovey. Right." Richard wiped the remaining dog spit from his mouth.

"So sorry. He's overly friendly and doesn't know his own strength. If I hadn't gotten here in time, I'm sure he would have-"

"Bitten my head off?"

The man cocked his head to the side. "Would have licked you to death."

Duke pulled again, his tongue lapping in and out of his mouth. He didn't look like a demon dog from that angle, but it sure felt like he was an attack animal when he stood his full weight on Richard's chest.

"Again, I'm so sorry," But the man didn't look sorry. He looked confused. As if Richard had said the wrong thing about his angel dog who had pushed him to the ground. "It won't happen again. I'll make sure Duke is on a leash just like his brother every time we go out for a-"

Richard braced himself for the next word.

"-walk."

Duke barked and pulled away from the man's grip again. He lunged with another bark, straight toward Richard. Yet another excited bark and again, the last thing Richard saw was the dog's barred teeth before he felt them nip his cheek.

"Oh, Richard!"

Just like that, the pain that should have come with Duke's bite to the face was non-existent. Amy's voice provided instant pain relief.

"Duke!" The man had pulled back his dog again. "I'm so sorry. Really, I am. I don't know what's gotten into him."

The man pulled Duke back several steps, still apologizing. "Really, sorry. I... it won't happen again."

But as the man's "sorries" and "reallys" faded down the sidewalk, Richard's eyes adjusted to the sunshine herself. Amy Jones was making her way down her steps and straight over to him. She was like Duke, running at full speed. But instead of slobber and teeth, she was full of concern and tenderness.

He leaned back, using his elbows as support, ready to bask in the rays she was willing to give.

"Oh my goodness, Richard! I heard all this noise outside. And I didn't want to be nosey, but I knew something was happening." She knelt down on the ground. Her perfect jeans dirtied at the knees. Yet, she didn't care. Who knows what kind of spit and dirt and bodily fluids were waiting for her there. And…she did not care.

Her entire focus was on Richard. Her wide eyes scanned his face, landing on his cheek. He was sure the dog left a mark, but he felt nothing. Not with Amy so close, making his butterflies crash into each other with excitement.

"Oh my goodness! I'm so glad I came out when I did. I'm so sorry it wasn't sooner. Maybe I…" She placed her hand on the side of Richard's face, and the touch electrocuted the butterflies.

"Maybe I could have prevented this."

The butterflies shattered when he saw the look on her face. She felt guilty. Her eyes sagged and her teeth bit her lip. He swore her cheeks flushed with heat. It was the damned dog's fault and she was holding onto the guilt.

"Come, let me help."

Her hand moved from his cheek to his elbow, and with every inch she moved her hand, he felt the butterfly pieces shutter and shiver back into place.

She lifted him off the ground and stood beside him, her hand wrapped around the crook of his arm as if it was built to fit there.

He didn't walk; he floated to her door. The butterflies lifted him up and took him there. They carried him inside and he was standing in her doorway, the front door closing behind him.

It was odd. Standing inside an apartment that was an exact replica of his, but completely different. The carpet was fluffed clean, vacuum marks still patterned against the fabric. The couch looked pristine. There were no greasy pizza stains on the cushions, no saggy butt craters from hours of watching mindless television, and it still had four matching pillows lining the back. This was still four more pillows than Richard ever had.

"Here, sit." Amy guided him down on the perfect couch.

He rested his hand over the couch arm, where it awkwardly landed on a small side table. Again, it was like his, only different. Better. Perfect.

Of course it would be perfect, not jammed and broken like his.

Amy disappeared into the bathroom, and Richard winced. Just two doors down; that's where he would spend moments thinking of her, touching himself, and filling his trash can full of soaked tissues and soiled toilet paper.

But she didn't know that. And that's definitely not what she was doing now.

Amy emerged from the bathroom, a handful of gauze and ointment and bandages.

That meant one thing. She was about to get a lot closer than she ever had to him. His butterflies smacked up against the walls of his stomach.

Richard felt the fabric on the couch shift as Amy sat down next to him. Her warmth spread to his side, filling him up with the magic of her sunshine.

"Here, let me see."

He didn't think it was possible, but she got even closer to him. She touched his cheek, gently turning his face so she could get a better look in the light.

"Tsk."

Even from this angle, he could tell her eyes were sad. They were sad for him. How he wanted to pull her into him, where they could melt into a tangle of a single body and make that sadness go away.

The butterflies reminded him: Amy Jones was not his to be had.

Amy sighed. "Okay. This might sting a little, okay?" She opened a bottle of hydrogen peroxide and tipped it over a pristine white cloth. Then, she brought it up to his cheek and dabbed it where Duke's teeth were just minutes ago.

It stung and bubbled, but Richard didn't pay the uncomfortable feeling any mind. He was busy watching her. The golden flecks in her eyes danced as her mouth formed a small O shape. Her breath cooled the stinging sensation and made his chest tighten up, choking out the butterflies, telling them not to move.

He wanted to get up, run, sprint out the door like he had the day he volunteered with the food drive.

But he also wanted to flip her onto her back, climb on top of her, and devour her skin from the tips of her ears to the end of her pinky toe.

He wanted to go back home, lock the door, close his eyes, and pretend like he didn't crave to breathe in the woman he couldn't have.

He wanted to scoop her up, melt her in his arms, and create tingles down her spine with his breath the way hers did to him.

Everything inside of him fluttered and looped and crashed and pulled, he couldn't decide what his body should do.

Then the front door swung open, freezing everything inside him including his breath.

"Oh, Neil, you're home!" Amy leapt from the couch and gave her husband a hug.

And yet, Neil's expression stayed on Richard.

He didn't smile. He didn't wrap his arms around the sunshine promised to him. He didn't say a word. He just stood there like a statue, not reciprocating the warmth his wife was willing to provide for him.

A single butterfly clipped its wings. If he couldn't have Amy Jones in the way he wanted, then neither should Neil or anyone else. Not if he wasn't going to be a cold statue toward her, toward this, toward the sunshine itself.

Richard tightened his fists. He could almost feel sticky red sauce squish within his palms, sticking his fingers together and oozing out between his knuckles. The possibilities of what they could do both filled him with excitement and chilled him to the core.

He had to get out of there before he could find out which feeling would win.

CHAPTER TWELVE

The strobing light from the living room blinds woke Richard up from his spot on the floor. At least this time, he was sure. This was home. This was *his* home. This was his familiarly sticky floor. The collection of alcohol bottles on the carpet were proof.

What would Amy think of that?

Flashes of the sunshine herself fluttered through memory.

Her arms wrapped around a cardboard box.

He wrapped his arms around himself.

Her fingers tucked back a piece of silken hair.

He rubbed his fingers together, pretending the lock was in his hands.

Her breath licked his cheek.

Lavender filled his nose, and his butterflies danced in aching circles.

Oh the way that woman pulled at him, and she had no idea.

And Neil. He may have chased her around the apartment like a game of cat and mouse, pinching her ass and spinning her in the air. But he also acted like a cold hunk of stone, standing there with unfeeling eyes and no reaction to her touch. Amy didn't deserve that.

His fists clenched together again and he swore he felt them stick together with anger and resentment. There was probably a teensy bit of jealousy, too.

Richard flung the bottle nearest him across the room and watched it shatter into glass confetti. Just as well. With an eviction hanging over him, it really didn't matter what happened to it.

It didn't matter.

The only thing that mattered was that he distanced himself away from Amy as fast as he could. If he took things into his own hands...

He found a second bottle, mostly empty, and chucked it angrily across the room, too. It hit the wall in almost the same place and shattered in sticky shards all over the floor.

Richard dragged himself off the carpet and to the bedroom, where his sheets lay crumpled in an abandoned nest. He grumbled as he kicked them aside. And again. Grumble. Kick. Grumble. Kick. There was no use for them anymore either. Right now, there was only one thing he had use for.

Well, a couple things. But he needed a box to fit them all.

He dropped to his knees at the bottom of his closet. "Where is it?" He grunted in frustration.

Empty hangers bounced off the closet walls, and forgotten clothes unstuck themselves from each other, emitting a musty odor in the air. Finally, his hand found the dry scratchiness of cardboard. He grasped its edge and pulled it out, avoiding an avalanche of closet debris.

Got it!

He went to work to fill it with anything worth a dime.

An old cell phone. A laptop he never used much anyway. A watch with a dead battery. He even threw in a few CDs and DVDs, though he wasn't sure who actually used those anymore.

Richard threw open the cabinet under the bathroom sink, where his power tools lived. In went a Dremel kit, electric screwdriver, and a jigsaw.

Slamming the cabinet shut, he thought of only one more thing worth pawning. The drawer on the little side table next to the couch was already open, waiting for the day Richard would fix the jam in the back. He shuffled his hands to the bottom of it, hoping he didn't misremember where he put it.

"Where is it?" He hissed out loud. As if his words conjured it into reality, his fingertips felt the ridged edge of a tiny coin. The cold metal shocked a memory wide open.

Richard's nine-year-old hand felt the embossed face in his hand. "A dime, Mom?" He stitched his eyebrows together. Why would his mom give him ten cents?

"Not just any dime, Richie. Take a look next to Roosevelt's face."

Roosevelt. He knew money all had the faces of dead presidents, but he could never remember who was who. He tried to etch Roosevelt's name into his memory so he could sound smart later.

He pinched the coin between his thumb and forefinger. With one eye closed, he examined the details. Nothing looked out of place to him. "I don't get it, Mom. This just looks like a regular dime."

He felt so impatient. Why was his mom giving him a dime anyway? This seemed like such a silly thing to bother him about. All he wanted was to bolt out of the front door and race down the street to play in the neighborhood creek and climb the big knotted tree in the corner. Break away from the house, away from his mom, and away from whatever special lecture this dime was going to bring out in her. She was good at that. Always coming up with some kind of special lesson over the littlest things. It would take a miracle for him to remember all the tiny lessons she gave him over things like piano keys, spaghetti sauce, and, now, a dime.

"Ah, that's the secret about it, Richie. Most things that are special don't look special. Not at first anyway. You can't always see what things are worth right away. But when you look closely, really closely, you'll find what makes even the tiniest thing special."

"So what's so special about a dime?" Richard rolled his eyes. He wished she would get to the point already.

"Well, this dime is special. It's not like most dimes. In fact, if you look again at Roosevelt, you might just see why."

Richard looked again. All he saw was the side of an old man's face. He let out a huff. "Mo-om." He was trying not to yell at her to hurry up. Every time he did, the lesson would take longer.

"Right here, Richie." Emily Teft pointed her manicured finger at the tiny letters reading, 'In God We Trust'.

He kept staring at it, hoping that whatever it was he was supposed to see would jump out at him and make itself known, but it didn't.

"Right here, there should be what's called a mint mark. It should be a letter 'P'."

Richard shook his head. "No, Mom, it's not there."

"That's the point, Richie. It should be there, but it's not. It's completely missing."

Emily Teft kissed her son on the top of his head. "No, Richie. It's not messed up. It's just a little different. The tiniest little piece makes it different from others that look just like it, which makes it special." She looked so proud of herself at that moment. "You'll see, when you get older, that things in life are a lot like this dime. You are like this dime. There's something that's just a little different that makes you special. Sometimes, those differences might even make things a little more valuable than you could even realize."

Emily gave him a knowing wink as if she expected him to take this as the key to understanding the rest of the world around him.

"But this dime is only worth ten cents."

Emily shook her head at him. "You still want to think it's worth ten cents because you've been told all things that look like a dime are worth only ten cents. But remember, a little difference could make all the difference in the world."

Richard's little mouth pursed in thought. "How much is it worth then?"

"Ah, if I told you, then you probably wouldn't believe me. I tell you what, hold onto it." Emily rolled her son's fingers around the coin. "You hold onto this for as long as you can, to remind you to keep looking for those tiny differences. Keep looking for what makes things special. When you find what's special about them, maybe you'll see the real value in it."

Richard used to look for the special thing in everything around him, from the stupid T-shirts he bought for himself to restaurant storefronts. The whole reason he applied to work as a backyard lumberjack was because their tagline was, **We use indus-tree-al strength**. At the time, he thought that was pretty special.

But after working with the crew for a few months, he realized it was just like any other job. The tagline was just a way to market to single moms who were wooed by bad dad jokes and families who wanted to expand their yard space on a budget. The magic of 'specialness' had dimmed just a little more.

At one point, curiosity did get the best of him, and he looked up the value of the coin itself. A quick search and he found it was worth a couple hundred dollars. Three hundred if he found the right place to sell. Between laziness and the lack of need, he never bothered to pawn it. Now was as good of a time as any.

Now, if he got the money he would be able to remove himself from Amy and whatever his hands wanted to do to her.

He tossed the coin in the box. It was just a *messed up* dime that happened to be worth more than ten cents. He grabbed the box with tentative hands and heard it clunk to the bottom. The butterflies knotted in his stomach as he brought it outside.

"Whatcha got in that box there, Richard?" A string of smoke slithered from Gladys's mouth.

Richard shook what was in his hands. Loose items rattled inside like old bones. "Oh, just some odds and ends."

"Odds and ends, you say?" Gladys stretched her neck forward, trying to get a look from her seat. "Looks more like a bunch of junk to me."

Richard sighed. "Odds and ends." It did look like he'd yanked out a forgotten junk drawer. His hope was a trip to trade out this clutter for a little bit of cash. That way, he could get the hell out of there and keep *her* safe.

"If you say so, Richard." Gladys eyed him cautiously. He could feel her foggy stare as he loaded the box in his truck. "You've got pawn shop eyes, Richard. Think you'll get enough to pay off your late rent?"

Richard sighed as he turned around and shrugged. "There's no rent to pay. That wasn't a warning. That was an eviction letter. The third this month, apparently."

"They're finally kickin' you to the curb, huh?"

"Guess so." Richard sucked in a deep breath of air. "This place never really felt like home anyway."

"Never *felt* like home? Richard, home ain't about a feeling. It's about having a place to sleep, eat, and piss without people watching you from the street. This is home, Richard. It's better than being out on your ass."

Richard leaned against his open car door and nodded. "A place to eat and sleep, huh? Yeah, well, I'm sure I'll find a place to do both of those without a problem. I can do any of that pretty much anywhere."

"Anywhere?" Gladys took another drag. "I've seen too many things to know *anywhere* isn't going to cut it. You'll need a solid footing, Richard. A place with four walls and a bed. *Anywhere* isn't going to give you that, you know."

"I'll make do, Gladys. Don't you worry about me."

You should be more worried about Amy, instead.

"I ain't the one to worry, Richard." Gladys tilted her head toward the right. "You know those two do enough of that for the rest of us. Don't let them hear about your *anywhere* plans. They'll end up putting you on their couch and raising a 'Save Richard Teft From Homelessness' fund until you get back on your feet." Gladys cackled at her own humor as she shook her head. When she finished, she looked him over. "Eh. I ain't worried about ya, Richard. I know you'll be fine. I just don't want it to be too quiet out here on the front porch. Who else am I gonna bug while I'm out here?"

"I'm sure you'll figure something out, Gladys."

With that, Richard climbed into his truck and shut the door. He may not have had an idea of where he'd end up, or what was next. But one thing was sure, he wasn't going to end up on Amy Jones's couch, fighting off his butterflies and fists until her dead body was at the bottom of his feet. He had to do what he could to get the hell out of there and keep *her* safe. The butterflies agreed.

The yellow lettered Pawn Shop sign loomed over Richard's truck from his parking space. He inhaled deeply and coughed it out, reminding himself that he'd be able to calm his nerves soon enough. Just a short trip in and out and he'd have enough to settle himself, afford to go somewhere else, and protect *her*.

Before he could let himself through the door, an intimidating voice stopped him in his tracks. "That's not what you said last week!"

Curiosity piqued, Richard cracked the door open to eavesdrop a little easier. A man as tall as Richard and slightly thinner stood in front of the counter. All Richard could see was the hood of his sweatshirt gathered at the back of his neck and a mop of dark hair on his head.

The man's fists were clenched by his side, the skin around his knuckles displaying splotches of white and red.

"Last week, you said I could pick it up for $200. Now you're just trying to rob me!" His heavy fist hit the counter.

Behind the counter, a stout man who resembled a biker stuck in the '80s wore a numbed expression. His arms crossed over his faded leather jacket, and Richard guessed from his stature this wasn't the first time he had seen this kind of behavior from a customer.

"I can't believe you're doubling the price on me! We had a deal, man. A deal!" Another fist hit the counter.

Still, the owner wore his blank expression proudly. He shrugged his shoulders. "Guys like you come in all the time, wanting something for nothing. Always claiming I said one thing one week and changing my mind on a whim the next. I'll tell you the same thing I tell them: I gave you the price — that's how much it costs. I can't change its worth just because you're throwing a temper tantrum. Take it or leave it. End of story."

"That is some *bull!*" The unhappy customer slammed both palms down with a *whack* and pushed his weight away from the counter in a huff. "Unbelievable *bull!*" He then covered his unruly mop with his hood and stomped his feet in a full-blown temper tantrum toward Richard.

As Richard edged himself through the door, he caught a glimpse at the customer's face under the loose hood.

"Neil?"

The man stopped, unclenched his fists, and pulled his hood down to reveal his quiet smile. "Oh, hi Richard." His voice cleared to his typical calming tone. The man he was just thirty seconds ago had faded away from sight. "Sorry you saw that, Richard. You know how these things go."

Richard shifted the box's weight in his hands. "Everything okay, Neil?"

"Oh yeah. You know, these places just aren't even worth the hassle. Trying to do something nice for someone else and they make it impossible." Neil rested a hand on Richard's shoulder and leaned in to whisper, "Don't let that guy take advantage of you, Richard. Make sure he gives you a good price and sticks to it." He slipped his hand away from Richard's shoulder and helped himself into the parking lot.

"Need a hand, there?"

"I'm good." Richard heaved the box up on the counter and began pulling out the top layer. As he laid his possessions on the counter top, the '80s biker popped open a small black box and slid a loose ring inside.

"What was that all about?" The words spilled out before Richard could dam a wall to keep them at bay.

"Oh that?" The man's eyes shifted to the front door. "Nothing. Happens nearly once a week. That guy was just hoping for a cheap ring. Guys like that want to make an impression on their lady without spending a dime." He lifted the box for Richard to see. "You see this? Black gold, blue topaz, 1.5 carats worth of diamond accents down the sides. And he thinks he can walk away with this for just a couple hundred? He's out of his mind."

The aftertaste of Neil's presence in the pawn shop sat uneasy with Richard. Why did he have the demeanor of a three-year-old in men's clothing? And how did he flip a mental reset switch the second he noticed Richard at the door?

He just wanted to buy something for Amy.

The rationalization came easy to him.

She deserves something nice once in a while, doesn't she?

She did. She deserved something nice all the time, no matter the cost.

But what if he couldn't afford it? What if it was out of range? What if he was told that there was absolutely no way he could give Amy Jones the one thing he wanted to?

Everyone has a breaking point. Maybe this was Neil's. Maybe this was the side of Mr. Jones that thawed out the cold statue and made him reciprocate his wife's warmth.

Pawn man snapped the box shut and slid it under the glass top. "So, what did you bring today?"

"Just some odds and ends."

"Anything you think we could sell here?" The man picked around inside as he eyed its contents.

Richard shrugged. "Maybe. I don't know." It felt like his throat was closing up on him. "Nothing like that ring, though. I can tell you that much.."

The ring smiled from the case under his arms. It really did look out of place, like the one nice thing in a mountain of forgotten trinkets and dust. It would look so damn nice on Amy's finger. It would have been *the* something special to be worn by *someone* special, and yes, she *should* have it.

A piece of Richard felt a little sorry for Neil. Too bad he didn't have the money to buy it either. If Neil couldn't afford it, there was no way Richard could. Not even if he emptied the last dime in his wallet and sold everything in the box in front of him. Even if he did, could he get away with buying it for *her*? Nah.

She wasn't his sunshine to be had.

The smell of aged leather brought Richard back to his senses. The man's arm had reached across him to lift out the tools on the top, nodding his head at each one. When he got to the power jigsaw and a well-used blade, he turned it over for inspection. "Looks pretty well used."

"Yeah, it is." Richard's eyes drifted back to the man. "It's always been trusty."

The man was clearly far more interested in the saw than anything else. He took his time turning it over in his hands and examining the teeth on the blade. As the man bobbed his head up and down, running his hand over the handle, Richard allowed his eyes to scan more of the room he was in.

His interest was in making sure whatever was in that box sold, so he'd let the man take his time

On his right was a coat rack weighed down by old leather and fur coats. Next to it was a knee-height white bench with a single pair of shoes: two well-worn black Avia's with cantilever soles. Richard shuffled his feet on the linoleum floor. They looked to be about his own size, 11.5. It was odd they were put on display nearly on a pedestal. He shrugged it off.

To his left, there was a small table with a clear plastic bin of baseball cards. No, not baseball cards. The handwritten sign read, *Serial killer trading cards*. Each one was laminated and labeled in white tape and black Sharpie. Soulless, faceless figures stared back at him from the top of the stack, and he wondered if there was a moment in time when they felt their conscience melt away from them or if they blinked and forgot their acts of violence.

On the wall behind the man at the counter was a collection of eerie paintings. The one in the middle caught Richard's attention and sent shivers crawling down his spine. A clown in a red striped suit and painted face. Something about it told him the artist himself was something from a child's nightmare to create the clown's off-center gaze and shaky lines.

This felt more like a secondhand serial killer warehouse than a pawn shop.

Above the crude painting hung a small boxed television, tuned to channel 5 news.

"Have you used it often?"

"Huh?" Richard's eyes stayed fixed on the television screen.

"This saw… have you used it?"

"Uh huh…" The sound was off, but Richard didn't need it on to know the story being reported.

He tried to cough up information about the saw to the man behind the counter to keep him from running back to his truck in search of a bottle he might have hidden away from himself.

"It's always been trusty."

A photo flashed on the screen.

"And here's the cord to it."

A beautiful blonde whose face was framed with tight curls.

"Powers up nice. It never failed.... me." Richard's voice faded into a choked breath. Another woman's photo displayed on the screen. This time, she was kneeling down next to a pink and black pig in front of the local community center.

Another woman. Another face in the parade.

It was the pig lady. The one who volunteered at the community center. The volunteer opportunity Amy had invited him to. He had gone. He had stood there, watching Amy introduce over-exhausted corporate employees to Porky and Piglet. She had led the monstrous animals to each tentative hand. And even though they were big and clumsy, she made it all look delicate. When she hugged Michelle at the end, he kept thinking about how their hair was the same. Both of their curls hit each other in a way where it was impossible to tell which ringlet belonged to which woman. Two women, arms wrapped around each other, with only one blonde mane.

The pawn shop owner hitched an eyebrow. "You never used this for anything other than home projects, right?"

"What?" Richard blinked his focus back to the pawn shop owner. "What else would I use it for?"

"You'd be surprised. People come in here all the time trying to get rid of power tools they used to murder their cheating wives or something crazy like that. Haven't you seen the news?"

Of course he had seen the news. He had seen the women's faces, read their names. He had burned their likeness into the back of his eyelids and tried to wash it away with alcohol. And yet, they were still there and they still kept coming. Of course he knew the news.

"I try not to pay any attention to it."

"You must be hiding under a rock, then, man." The man grabbed a nearby remote and flicked his wrist over his shoulder. The sound on the TV behind him grew loud enough to hear the reporter, but Richard's own thoughts fought to drown out the individual words.

The reporter droned on about the woman in the picture. Snapshots of her house blanketed the screen. Women with reddened eyes made guest appearances. One of the pink and black pigs grazed in the yard behind the reporter.

Richard felt his chest stiffen and his breath shake. The butterflies were struggling to make any movement.

The reporter continued on, including snapshots of Leslie Arlene.

His breath came quick and shallow. His eyes burned with fear, and he swore the pawn shop owner could feel his butterflies in the air around him.

He swallowed the lump that had formed in his throat. "No, nothing like that. Just, you know, cutting up pieces of wood and stuff. But if there's someone doing that kind of stuff around here, maybe I should keep it on hand." Maybe it *would* be better for him to keep the saw in his own hands. Maybe he could protect himself… or someone else… maybe it would help him protect Amy.

"They're calling him the Samhale Strangler. He just broke into these women's houses and snuffed them out with a pillow or something. Guess you're pretty safe carrying around a jigsaw for now. That ain't his M.O. Not yet." The man scratched his chin. "I'll give you $13 for it."

"What do you mean?"

"You askin' about his strangling or what I'll take for your stuff?"

Richard already regretted his question. "Either, I guess."

"Well, they haven't figured out exactly what's going on. But it won't take long before he gets bored with taking the air outta people's lungs. When that happens, he'll end up escalating."

"Escalating?"

Could he do worse?

"Yup. To something like this." The man held up the jigsaw. "Thirteen dollars?"

"How do you know?" Richard gulped. Could his own hands do worse?

The other man shrugged. "It's just what they do before they get caught. They start out as peeping Toms."

Outside Amy's apartment, was that what he was doing? No. That was not what it felt like at the time. Peeping Toms were creeps who wanted to knock their rocks off by sneaking peeks that weren't meant for them. Looking inside Amy's window was just...satisfying his curiosity.

"Then when window-watching doesn't work for them anymore, they try something else."

Richard's stomach tied in knots as moments of blackouts ran past his memory.

"And if it's something like that," he pointed to the TV, "it won't take long before he moves on to feel the blood on his hands."

Richard's butterflies nearly strangled each other, begging for a break from what they were hearing, and his throat felt like it was collapsing on itself. He could feel tendrils of hair around his fingers and tried to push away the image of holding Emily Teft in his arms and red sauce sticking to his fingers. He took a shaky inhale and wished he could swallow down something more than air.

"So… thirteen for the saw. A quarter for each of the DVDs and CDs. Fifty for the old iPhone if it's in working order. And… twenty for the rest of the lot."

Richard's attention drifted to the pawn shop man's hands. He had placed the jigsaw back into the box and was thumbing through the pile of DVD cases in front of him, ensuring each one included the correct disk inside.

Before Richard could tell his hands not to, they wrapped around the box and hugged it close to him. His feet acted on impulse, too, backstepping toward the door. The sound of the dime dragging at the bottom of the box was like a drumroll to when his chest would stop working all together.

"Hey, don't you want the money for this stuff here?" The man gestured back and forth from the scattered items left on the counter to the box Richard held in his hand. He looked as confused as Richard felt.

"No. Um. No thanks. You keep that. Um. Thank you." His feet continued to move until he felt his back hit the long handle of the door. He pushed it open, giving the man a strained smile as he left the shop.

As cool as the air outside felt on his face, it still tasted stale in his strained breaths. He had to find a way to breathe. And he had to get out of there. Not just the shop, but out of Bridgewell, away from Amy before the butterflies left his body and strangled her for taking his breath away.

CHAPTER THIRTEEN

The police cars looked strange, just sitting there on the side of the road without their lights on. Movies and TV shows always showed those kinds of cars racing down the street with the lights on full blast. The same went for the ambulance and fire trucks. They were always loud and interrupted the characters from whatever they were doing — in mid conversation, having dinner, or doing that *thing* that grown-ups do together in their bedrooms behind closed doors. But these cars were quiet and dark, like they weren't awake at all.

There was also a big, long car that didn't look like it had lights at all. That one came and left a long time ago. She had watched a bed-like thing get rolled out of the house and loaded into the back of it. She didn't want to think about what was hiding under the cloth that was on top of it. After watching the creeping man, she could guess what was under there, and it made her stomach feel like the time she ate a bowl of *Froot Loops* with spoiled milk.

The police had stuck around for a while, though. They were still here, talking to one another in hushed voices and coded words. Seven of their cars were parked outside while the men in suits were pacing in and out of the house. She made sure to keep her back to the old tree while she watched. That tree always made her feel uneasy whenever she saw it, now more than ever. If she were facing it, there's no way she'd be able to think about anything else other than the creeper man who was singing nursery rhymes walking out of the woods. Her gaze stayed in front of her to make sure her focus was on the commotion in front of her instead.

One police officer was standing close to the road only a few feet away from her. He was tall and thin, reminding her of the man on the TV show her mom watched, who was always wearing a suit and a serious face. Her mom always made weird googly eyes when he was on the screen.

The man in front of her stood still as if he was waiting for something to happen in front of him. Really, in front of both of them, but he didn't know she was there. If he did, he'd probably shoo her away like most grown-ups did. She wanted to reach out to him, touch his suit, and ask all the questions that were buzzing in her head like static.

What happened? Did they catch the creeper man? If there were this many police cars and a long dark car that picked up a bed, then the lady inside was definitely hurt. How badly was she hurt? She didn't want to admit to herself how bad it must have been, though, because that would turn the creeper man into something much, much worse, and she wasn't ready to handle having that kind of grown-up information.

The policeman near her called on his walkie-talkie. It sounded like a bunch of numbers that didn't make any sense, but something in his voice made her believe he was concerned. It was like he wanted to apologize and cry about the codes he was giving out. When he was done talking into it, he called over another policeman to ask him for an update. This one was short and round, the exact opposite of the thin policeman her mother would make googly eyes at if given the chance.

"It's another of his," the round man said. "Everything seems to fit. Well, almost everything. The only thing is that the M.O. is slightly different." He scratched at his patchy beard.

His? M.O?

"What do you mean different?" the first policeman asked.

What does he mean by another of the same?"

"I mean, it was asphyxiation, but she also has a laceration running from the back of her hand to her elbow."

Asphyxiation? Laceration? What did those mean?

All the questions buzzed inside of her.

"He cut her?"

Finally, an answer. Laceration must mean cut. She'd have to ask about that other big word.

"Seems like it."

"Shit. But not to kill her?"

Did he or didn't he kill her?

"Do you know anyone who'd die of an arm cut?"

The tall man crossed his arms. "That depends. How deep is the cut?" His voice sounded serious, much like when her mom asked about something that happened at school when the teacher already called home to tell her what happened.

"Not deep enough for that. It was definitely asphyxiation that did her in."

She found herself inching closer to both of the men. Their conversation was adding up to a lot of question marks, and she couldn't help herself from wanting to insert her nose and get something answered. Maybe they could help her iron out her confusion, give her some kind of understanding as to what she had seen. Or hadn't seen. She unlatched her helmet and approached the man with hesitation.

"So does that mean he killed her?" Her voice felt tiny coming out into the open, but she could tell they had heard her. Both men turned around with wide, surprised eyes. Little owls, themselves. They were caught with their hands in the cookie jar, and she was going to figure out what kind of cookies they were dealing with.

The tall policeman looked down at her, brows furrowed and lips pinched. "Well, that's not something you hear from most little girls, is it?"

"No, sir. It's not. But I'm not like most little girls." She hoped she pulled off her authoritative tone. "I'm also not so little."

He chuckled at her. "No, I suppose you're not." He looked above her head, eyes scanning behind her, and she had a feeling he was searching for an adult that she belonged to.

"If you're looking for my mom, she's not here. Well, not *here* here. But that doesn't really matter. I'm old enough to be out on my own as long as I stay on the roads I know and come back home when she says it's time."

"Ah. I see. Well, can I suggest that you go on ahead, then? This really isn't a place for little girls to be."

She twirled her helmet in her hand. "I know I'm not supposed to argue with a cop, but, sir," she wrung her hands together, "this is exactly where kids are all the time. And again, I'm not so little." She mumbled the last part under her breath.

"Excuse me?" His widened eyes grew even wider.

She pointed to the gnarly tree with a shaky finger. "That's where we play. The kids in the neighborhood, that is. Sometimes, anyway. We climb up that creepy tree and pretend like there's a treehouse that was built just for us. No grown-ups allowed or anything." She bit her bottom lip. "At least that's what it's like when I'm with them."

"Oh, I see. That's not exactly what I—"

"But I'm not always with them. In fact, I'm hardly ever with them. They like to play little kid games while up in that tree. And sometimes that gets a little boring. I might be a kid, but I'm not a *little* kid." She saw his face. He pinched it up like he was annoyed at her for cutting him off. Before he could shoo her away, she continued. "I know what you meant, though. Here. Like, in front of this house, with seven police cars and the creepy long car that took away… that thing. This isn't a place for kids like me."

He nodded his head. "That's exactly what I mean." His face was less annoyed now.

She scrunched up her face. He still hadn't answered her question. "So, is that what it means, though? As-fixy-a-ton? Did the creeper man kill the woman who used to live here?"

The policeman knelt down to her level and looked her in the eye. He had piercing blues that looked sad. Now she was really sure her mom would have made googly eyes at him.

"Listen, do you know how police stuff works?" he had asked in his gruffly, kind voice.

She nodded her head. "Yeah, you work to stop bad guys from doing the stuff they're not supposed to be doing. Bad stuff. Sometimes *really* bad stuff. And when you can't find them, you make it your job to find them first and then stop them."

He nodded back. "Yes, and we also work to protect the good guys. Good guys like, well, like you." He pointed his index finger at her. "So part of my job is to make sure you're safe."

"Does that mean you caught the bad guy then? Did he do really bad stuff?"

He sighed at her questions. "It means I can't really answer your questions. All the information we have, it needs to stay with us." He looked uncomfortable, like he was standing in shoes a size too tight.

The round officer spoke up, "It's grown-up information we need to handle and you don't need to worry about, okay? We promise, once we collect all the grown-up information we can, we'll be able to stop this bad guy and all the other bad guys."

"All the others?" Her mind went racing like a bullet. "How many are there?"

The tall officer sighed and crouched down to her level. "Not enough that we can't get them, kid."

She cocked her head to the side. "So does that mean there is a bad guy around here right now?"

His mouth turned down at her question. "I can't answer that either, kiddo. Like I said this is all—"

"Yeah, yeah, it's grown-up information. I got it." She had already regretted poking her nose into their conversation. She was getting nothing. Nada. Zilch. It was more of the secrets that were being kept from her.

"Right. Look, why don't you go on home? Hang out with your mom and do something fun, you know? Just make sure you go straight there, okay? And don't talk to—"

"Yeah, yeah. Don't talk to strangers." She rolled her eyes. They weren't taking into account that police officers were just as much strangers as anyone else.

"Exactly. Don't talk to strangers. Especially ones that are suspicious."

Suspicious. Out of all the nothing they gave her with their words, this was one that had something.

Suspicious. She'd keep that in mind, be on the lookout, make a note if she saw anything that looked *suspicious*.

She gave him a salute from her forehead and felt like she was on official business doing so. Finally, something she could use.

CHAPTER FOURTEEN

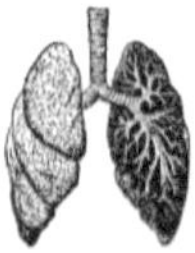

Lying in bed, he felt his chest tighten close. There it was, that same feeling he had been struggling with for who knows how long. There was nothing visible actually strangling him, yet it still felt like his windpipes were closing by force. He gave it all his might. But only a thin sliver of oxygen went through his nose. Visible or not, he knew what that force was.

This was it. He had had enough. All the times before never did him any long term good. But this time, he had to have *her*.

Gingerly, he slipped one foot out of bed. His big toe reached the floor first. Then, one by one, his other toes reached the shag carpet. He slipped his other foot to do the same, and a ripple of goosebumps covered his body. He tiptoed across the room, trying to keep his excitement as locked up as his airways were.

This was it. This was going to be it. He couldn't believe he was finally going to be free after all this time.

He blinked and found himself in the kitchen. It was like his body had brought him there without his mind making it happen. *Thank you*, he thought. His body was making it easier by running on autopilot.

The calendar glared at him from its place on the wall. All the little squares with tick marks and reminders scrawled in black and red marker looked like maddening chicken scratch. It reminded him of how his head felt — as if someone took a pen to it to scratch out all the logical thoughts, leaving behind a messy tangle of emotions in their place.

The sight made him choke on air all over again.

He needed out. And there was no time to waste.

No, not out; he needed to *breathe*. He needed to open his airways for good this time. And it would have to be from *her*. That was the only thing that made sense.

How many times had he been here in the kitchen, in search of a late night snack, only to find nothing in the fridge he wanted? Too many to count. It was never food he needed anyway. He had just been pacifying the time until he could scratch the itch that had been digging at him. This time, he wasn't even going to bother with the fridge. This time, he was looking for something above it. He was going to scratch that itch and be done with it for good.

He opened up the cabinet above the fridge and reached in blindly with his hand. Bottle. Bottle. Bottle.

Stupid little soldiers.

Jackpot.

In a world where everything else was labeled with someone else's name and needs, this was the one thing that was truly his own: The faded pillowcase with blue lavender flowers and the scent of a thousand women. Well, maybe not a thousand, but it was enough he had lost track.

He pulled it from its home in the cabinet and lifted it to his face. He took a deep inhale of the fabric. The scent of vanilla and lavender shampoos that lingered within the threads opened his airways just enough not to be painful.

Yes. This was helpful. This is what he needed.

He opened it up and felt the inner layer. The sticky plastic clung to his fingers as he touched it. No air was going in and out, especially after his last patching job. But this wouldn't be enough. Not for *her*.

She needed something grander, bigger.

An idea hit him. The hallway closet held so much potential. It was where forgotten bags and fabrics hid as the more well-worn coats lived on hangers. He helped himself to the door and dropped to the floor. On his hands and knees, he searched around for it.

Shoes. Empty coathangers. Sweaters that had long ago fallen to the floor to collect dust.

Ah, there it was. A large duffle bag that had carried *her* spare clothes and supplies for so many years. It had served its use so many times before, but he had one more job left to do.

He laid the bag on the floor and assessed its size. It wasn't big enough for an entire body.

That could be problematic. But what if that body wasn't whole?

His arm would fit inside okay. So if his limbs would fit, there was definitely enough room for *her* dismembered parts.

His butterflies danced in rapid motion. The grand finale would be so… grand.

He eased the bag onto his shoulder and put the pillowcase inside. There was one more thing he needed, and it was in a tiny drawer in the side table by the couch.

He pinched the small knob and eased the drawer open. Even in the darkened room, he could tell where the handle was. His fingers remembered where it was without hesitation. He wrapped his hand around it and gripped it tight. It felt powerful, like it could do anything he wanted. And if this knife could cut through beef bones like butter, imagine what it could do to a human's.

A vibration in his back pocket alerted him to a message. He was glad he remembered to turn off the ringer this time. Pulling his phone out of his pocket to check the screen, a jolt of energy ran through him.

A: **I miss you. Ready to play?**

The corners of his mouth twisted up. He would be ready. Soon.

With the materials in hand, he was ready. He would finally have *her*, in the only way he had ever wanted.

Amy Jones was his for the taking, and so was her last breath.

Then, he could play.

CHAPTER FIFTEEN

Richard Teft gazed out of his truck window, the engine still purring its tune. He tried to make sense of the image in front of him, but he couldn't figure it out. He had left Bridgewell apartments behind without any idea of where the road would take him. All he knew was that he had to be out. Gone. Away. Left out of Amy Jones's existence.

He didn't plan on driving back to the work site where Good 'ol Dave last told him to go sober up. The memory struck Richard as funny, sitting there with a box full of tiny alcohol bottles rattling in the passenger's seat next to him. He had raided his apartment for the stash he hid from himself in case of an emergency.

He killed the ignition and hoisted himself out of the truck. Leaning against its side, he contemplated the view. That large oak tree was still there. Its thick trunk stood strong in the house's backyard by itself, thanks to Dave and the crew chopping down whatever else had been there. The lawn was pock-marked with multicolored leaves. The branches stuck out, like arms open wide, inviting him over. If he squinted, the knotted bark looked like a face staring back at him. It looked as curious about him as he was of it. He swore if he focused his ears enough, he could hear it calling him over.

"Watch out, mister!"

A blur of red and black whizzed by him.

"Whoa, hey boy! Watch where you're going. You're going to run into somebody speeding by like that." Richard uncrossed his arms and stood up straight. That kid needed to be careful.

The kid moved a foot off the skateboard to stop it from rolling. Then, he picked it up and turned to face Richard. "I ain't no boy, mister." She pulled her black and red helmet off her head, revealing two blonde pigtails tied in pink ribbons.

No; she wasn't a boy. She was a miniature version of the familiar faces he had seen on the news.

Richard's cheeks flushed. How many blondes could possibly live in Samhale? "Oh, um. Sorry. I didn't mean…"

Pigtails shook with her head. "No one ever does." She sucked in her cheeks and furrowed her brows. She was taking him in the same way Gladys took in her cigarettes — like she was sucking in judgment so she could puff out a response later.

The butterflies jumbled together, uncomfortable. A kid shouldn't be out, alone, staring down a stranger with judgmental eyes. She should have a parent around somewhere to advise her to move on, skate past this man. Don't talk to strangers and all that.

Richard looked at the quiet houses around them. "So … where's your mom?" He was a terrible judge of age. Her height told him she was no older than nine. But the way she carried herself and with the confidence that radiated off her, she seemed a lot older.

"I ain't supposed to tell no one that. Suppose she's down the block out of eyesight and you were to throw me in that truck of yours." She spat on the ground. "Or suppose she's right there in the house you're parked in front of, staring out the window. Watching you. Waiting to call the cops in case you do try nabbing me."

Richard's palms broke into a sweat. This kid was confronting. Head on. There was nothing wishy-washy or people-pleasing about her.

"How come I ain't never seen you around here before?" The girl kicked up her skateboard and held it upright in her free hand.

"I, um…" Richard wasn't sure what to tell her. In a neighborhood like this, everyone probably knew everyone else. They probably held block parties where they trade off barbeques and macaroni recipes. They probably had a neighborhood watch to keep an eye out for suspicious behavior and gave out spare keys to one another whenever they went out of town. "You're probably too busy riding that board of yours." Richard felt the handle of his truck door with a sweaty hand. Oh how he wished he could grab another bottle from the box in his seat and replace the heat of his palms with liquid heat down his throat.

The kid crossed her arms at him. "I notice lots of stuff, mister, and I ain't never noticed you." She paused, looking at him with that Gladys look again. "Nope. I'm sure of it. If you'd have been around here before, I would have noticed. But you haven't. You're new around here, and I haven't had the chance to figure you out yet."

A sharp knot ran down Richard's throat. The only thing he had figured out about himself was that he needed out of Bridgewell and to somewhere he could keep *her* safe from his hands.

Pigtails bounced against her temple as she tossed her head toward the house behind her, the empty one with a for-sale sign in the front yard. The one she supposed her mom could be in, watching over her. "You doin' somethin' with that house, mister?"

Richard cocked an eyebrow. "I thought you said your mom was in there, watching over you." He hadn't noticed the for-sale sign before.

The girl threw her skateboard down and secured her helmet in place. With a foot on the board, she shrugged her shoulders. "She still could be, but I ain't tellin' you that. Strangers ain't supposed to know nothin' personal about me." She furrowed her brows at him. "My eyes are open, mister, and I'm keepin' them on you." With squinted eyes, she secured her helmet back on her head and sped off on four wheels.

What a strange kid.

Richard breathed out a sigh of relief. No one was in that house. There was no one there watching over him, wondering what an unwashed man in his thirties was doing in the middle of this suburban street, staring out into a random yard. At least that was what it looked like from where he stood. With an empty driveway, dark windows, and a sign advertising its sale, he was pretty sure it was empty. And even if there were someone inside, watching his every move, he wasn't here for any kid. He was there for something else entirely. His eyes gazed forward at the wide oak tree. Its branches spread out toward all sides, welcoming him over, calling him home.

Home?

A place to eat and pee in peace.

A quick look left and right to assure himself no traffic was coming, Richard walked toward it, drawn to it like a siren's call. Once the trunk was within reaching distance, his hand magnetically reached out to touch it. The rough bark scratched his skin, but it felt solid. This tree felt strong, protective. Like it was meant to be there to keep him safe. Walking around the tree, he surveyed its roots. Before running underground, they tied themselves in knotted tendrils, crossing in and out of each other like wooden snakes. He sat on one that arched up, acting like a private seat just for him.

He ran a hand to the knotted root in front of him. There was an aged carving, little slash marks someone made with a knife years ago. He explored the notches, and he swore he felt the oak tree shudder from pain. The cold feeling shocked through his fingertips and ran all the way to his spine.

Continuing his way around the tree's trunk, he found a large, hollow opening. The bark had split ages ago, and Richard imagined as the oak grew in size, it accepted the hole as part of itself.

He had been wrong before. The side from the street wasn't the tree's face. This was. The hollow gaped open, like a mouth calling out, but since it faced away from the road, no one but Richard would see it. It was his secret to keep.

He marveled at the massive gaping, wondering if he were slightly thinner and a lot shorter, if he could slip himself inside. Had he tried to worm his body into it, he probably could have made it work. But there was a more comfortable option for him to take. One that would allow the gaping hole to stay open, ready to call out to him whenever she needed.

She.

Maybe it was the changing color of leaves that reminded Richard of the way a woman's hair falls on her shoulders. Or it could have been the slight vanilla scent that reminded him of a woman's sweet fragrance. He liked to think it was the way the tree held him that made him believe he knew the tree was a woman.

"Hi," he whispered to her, and instantly felt ridiculous. If anyone had heard him, he'd earn a quick title of 'the crazy man in the truck', which wouldn't be too far off from the truth. But he didn't want to speed that conclusion up.

A quick look at the road told him the kid wasn't there anymore. Neither was anyone else. It was a rush of relief to know no one was watching him or listening in on a one-sided tree conversation. "Guess it's just you and me, huh?"

The wind blew quickly through the leaves, and he swore he heard a whisper back. *"Climb."*

Without thinking, Richard's muscles went to work. Their memory for climbing was still strong, even without a harness or a group of men yelling at him to do it 'right'. His left hand would wrap around a branch, then his right on one slightly higher. He'd stretch and pull himself a little at a time.

"Climb."

One more heave and he was another foot higher.

"Climb."

His feet found security in the crooks and curves in each lifted step.

"Climb."

He pulled himself to a sitting position in the middle of the open branches, allowing his feet to dangle over the side. It felt like he was a child being cradled in loving arms.

"Home," the whisper told him.

"Home," he whispered back. This, he could get used to.

With nowhere to go and no one expecting him, Richard allowed himself to sit until the sun shifted several positions in the sky. He watched birds come and go, sharing his branches in brief moments. The leaves shook every time one tweeted past as if it were waving them goodbye, wishing someone would stay longer.

I will. I'll stay.

In the not quite fading sun, Richard shot a look toward the back of the house. There was a large pile of lumber sitting not-so-nicely next to a freshly built back porch. Home renovations that were finished, but the leftovers were never cleaned up.

"How long has that been there?" Somehow talking to his tree, his voice didn't feel so strained. The words fell out of him naturally, like breathing.

"Build," the whisper answered.

"Build." He nodded. "Okay. I see."

Richard helped himself down from the tree and made his way to the pile. The top piece was slightly warped. He knew from experience these were boards that had bowed in the hardware store. The contractors probably saved them for last, hoping to not have to use them. Regardless, this was still good, pressure-treated wood. It would still work.

It would still create the home he needed.

The sun shifted again in the sky as he pulled piece by piece over to the oak, to *her*. With each board he carried, the light dimmed another notch and her leaves rustled in anticipation.

"I understand. Just a little longer," he reassured *her*.

Richard wasted no time when the last board joined the pile. His arms provided everything he needed to make measurements. From wrist to elbow was a foot. Thumb to forefinger was 6 inches. He pulled a pen from his back pocket and marked them one by one until his eyes couldn't break through the darkening sky any more.

Fumbling through his box he brought with him, he pulled out a tiny bottle of liquid warmth. He was too tired to care about what was on the label or how it would hit his taste buds. His back settled against the pile of wood, feeling the sharp edges support his back in a slumped position. The bottle's rim hit his mouth and he sucked it dry, satisfied with himself and the tree who was accepting him. He allowed his eyes to close into darkness when he addressed the oak once more.

"Sorry, Amy. Just a little while longer."

CHAPTER SIXTEEN

The nighttime breeze felt good against her face. If it weren't for her determination, that breeze would be her favorite part of her outings. But the *bumpbumpbumpbumpbump* of the wheels under her feet kept her mind and eyes wide open. The grown-ups always talked about wanting to put together something called a 'neighborhood watch', but no one actually stepped up to do it. So if the grown-ups weren't going to do anything about it, then she darn well would.

That was the absolute best part about her nightly adventures. She was doing something about it, even if none of the grown-ups really knew. Not that they needed to. If they did, they'd try to stop her and then nothing would get done.

There was a weird man in the neighborhood now. That made two people out when they shouldn't be. With the creeper she saw a couple nights ago and the police at the house by the tree that freaked her out, there was something going on. Something bigger than the non-Mr. Beasley showing up to Mrs. Beasley's house. Her eyes were open to full power now, pretending she was an owl, flying down the road on her skateboard.

The autumn wind blew again, and leaves spilled into the air. The noise they made hitting each other sounded like they were chattering about the secrets the night held. Those secrets wouldn't be kept from her for too long. She was bound to unlock them for herself.

The grown-ups wouldn't let her know whatever it was they knew. *If* they even knew anything at all. There was no way she'd let the stupid trees keep secrets from her, too.

She didn't even get to Beacon Road, which meant this would have been a short trip. It also would have meant it would have been a boring one, too. But movement by that really weird tree caught her attention, which made it not-so-boring after all.

That tree always looked funky to her. The roots stuck out in crazy directions, and the tree trunk was so old the bark stuck out like week-old scabs falling off your knee. It always looked like an old bumpy face staring back, ready to pounce at any moment. There were times she imagined it would open a mouth and start screaming. Whenever her imagination played that kind of trick on her, she'd skate a little faster to go past it, trying her hardest not to look back.

She stopped herself right by the white truck. The same one she saw earlier that day. It should have driven off somewhere, to that guy's home, maybe. Wasn't that what grown-ups did? They went back home before it turned night to tuck themselves in for their early mornings. But it didn't. He didn't. It was parked right in front of that old man tree, and that was just weird.

No one was inside the truck. She knew because she looked inside the window out of curiosity. Not even the funny-smelling guy who called her a boy. She wrinkled her nose. He didn't seem very smart, but she couldn't be sure. If there was a reason he was there — like the way the policemen were — then his parked truck might have made more sense. But he was no policeman. Policemen were clean and wore uniforms. And they didn't look her in the eye when she asked them questions they didn't want to answer.

She wanted to know more about this man, but she didn't want to let this guy know anything about her, especially where she lived. That was Keep Yourself From Being Kidnapped 101. Don't tell a stranger where you live. Saying her mom was maybe in that house and maybe not might have confused him enough not to connect any dots. Grown-ups didn't always catch onto the truth if you got all screwy with the details.

Her mom was nervous about whatever was going on. She knew that much. Every time she walked into a room with the TV on or her mom's cell phone open to a new photo, Mom shooed her away. "Go find something fun to do, Mills. This is nothing for little girls to worry about." Her mom was never quick enough to turn it off, though. She still saw them — all the women's faces that were all over the news. If they all stood in a line together, it could be like taking a family photo.

They were all blonde women with curly hair, just like her mom. Just like her.

She could almost picture her mom's face displayed with the others. That was enough to confirm that her nighttime strolls were important. If this wasn't something that little girls should worry about, then all the grown-ups wouldn't walk around like they were openly scared of their own shadows. That kind of thing is exactly what made girls like her sneak out of her bedroom window to go hunting for secrets.

Another gust of wind and more leaves flew out of the trees. The big, funky tree in front of her had fewer leaves on its branches now, which made it look even crazier than before. It was always kind of like a fat skeleton, but now it was like a balding fat skeleton, fading its age with time.

More movement by the tree reminded her why she was there. There the shadow was, creeping toward the tree's large trunk.

The creeper from the other night. It had to be him. Who else could it have been?

Pulling her knees up to her chest, she focused on keeping her eyes open and unblinking to see what would happen.

The shadow carried a large bag. The kind that her mom brought with her when she packed for the gym, only bigger. And from the looks of it, it was heavier, too. The shadow was dragging it with both hands. She could tell because of the way the shadow was walking, like it was dragging itself first before dragging the bag behind it on the ground.

She couldn't tell where the shadow came from before it was at the tree, but it was probably from the woods behind the house. Or what was considered woods. It was really just a clump of smaller trees that separated the houses on this street from the houses on the street behind it. Just enough to go unseen but not enough to get yourself lost in. It made sense he would come from there. It would have been pretty stupid for someone to drag a heavy bag along the road like that. The pavement would have ripped a hole in the bottom of it. At least, that was what had happened to her backpack the year before. She didn't feel like carrying it from the bus stop, so she dragged it all the way home. Boy, Mom was mad at her for the hole she made from doing that. She never dragged anything on the road after that time. Not even her shoes.

The creeper shadow stopped moving by the tree trunk. There was a pile of something on the ground, but she couldn't tell what it was. It made a weird sound when the creeper kicked it. Kind of like a mix between hitting her dresser with her bare foot and dropping a handful of her books at the same time. It kind of sounded painful, but the creeper shadow didn't yell out like he was hurt or anything.

The shadowy figure moved toward the back of the tree trunk where she couldn't see what was going on. Even moving herself around to the other side by the passenger's door, she couldn't tell what the figure was doing. It didn't help that the moonlight wasn't bright tonight. She spat at the ground, wondering why nighttime clouds had to make it difficult for her.

Owl eyes, she reminded herself. *Keep your owl eyes open.*

She didn't dare move closer. She knew walking on the leaves in the grass would make too much noise, and she didn't want to let this creeper know she was sneaking around, keeping her eyes on him.

The *zrriiip* of a zipper put her ears on high alert. She imagined the shadowy figure unzipping the bag and opening it wide before him, the way her mom did after a day at the gym. It always smelled funny when she did that. An unhappy grunt came from behind the tree. Maybe whatever was in the bag smelled funny, too.

A man's voice came after the grunt. From where she was, she couldn't make out all the words, but they came in sing-songy spurts. Grunt. Word. Grunt. Word. Grunt. To her, it sounded something like "You. Must. Love. Me." or "To. Trust. Glove. Pee."

It probably wasn't the last thing. Unless the creeper wasn't just a creeper. He could have been a crazy man, too. You never can tell these days.

She shrugged it off and kept her eyes open, hoping to figure out more of the creeper's secret behind the tree.

Another grunt. She swore she heard something else with it. Something squashy that made her nose turn up and her stomach feel like it wanted to empty out the spaghetti dinner her mom served up hours ago. She held it back, though. Spaghetti throw-up was the worst kind, and spilling her guts on the side of the road was a good way for her to get caught.

That ain't happening.

After the sound that made her stomach turn, there was another *zrriip*. She imagined her mom zipping up her gym bag after unloading the dirty clothes from inside. Now empty, and probably still stinking up the insides. She never could understand how her mom could stand carrying around a bag that smelled so bad all the time.

The shadowy creeper moved away from the back of the tree and kicked the pile a second time. Again, she heard the painful dresser-kick-falling-books sound.

The bag must have been a lot lighter now, because the creeper wasn't dragging it on the ground anymore. He carried it over his shoulder without any effort and disappeared into the woods. A quick "Diddle diddle" sing-songy sound drifted from the trees to her ears.

That was weird.

She flipped her skateboard upside down so it wouldn't roll away and took slow steps toward the tree. Her curiosity about the pile on the ground wanted to be settled. Another step closer and she rubbed her eyes to help them focus. Wood? Wood and a pile of clothes?

But before she could investigate closer, she heard some muttering from the woods behind the house. Not muttering. Singing. Singing loudly.

"Lavender's green, diddle diddle. Lavender's blue."

It was the nursery rhyme her mom used to sing to her when she was little, right before bed. But something felt off about a grown man's voice singing it from the woods behind the house. At night. With a bag of *something* over his shoulders.

"You must love me, diddle diddle. Cause I love you."

Nope. She needed out of there. A man singing nursery songs out in the open in the middle of the night wasn't going to catch her sneaking around, watching him do whatever it was he was he shouldn't be doing.

She booked her tail back to the truck, holding the skateboard by the wheels. Effortlessly, she flipped it right side up on the road and hopped on, leaving the shadow and his creepy little song behind her.

"I heard one say, diddle diddle, since I came hither. That you and I, diddle diddle, must lie togetherrrrr."

As she sped away on her skateboard, the voice grew clear behind her. The windpipes of this creeper man were ready and prepped, like he wasn't keeping a secret from anybody any longer. That freaked her out. Grown-ups were used to keeping their secrets in the dark. She wasn't ready to find out what this creeper's secret was and why he was breathing it out into the open so freely. Not this way. Not face-to-face with the creeper himself.

Not yet, anyway. The secret would come out eventually. And when it did, she would be there to bust it wide open. In her way. On her terms. With grown-up information in her hands.

CHAPTER SEVENTEEN

The chilly morning breeze shook Richard awake. He blinked his eyes several times to make sense of his surroundings. Leaves. Open air. Birds. Bark. As many times as he had woken up in odd places before, this wasn't one of them. He was right where he was supposed to be. Home.

He smacked his lips together. They were dry, cracked. That would need to be fixed. But when he stood up and stretched, pain shot through his side. Bending over to lift and carry several boards of lumber would do that to a person. Passing out on those same wooden boards probably didn't do him any favors, either. A warm drink would definitely help him feel better.

He eyed the pile. Last night, he got halfway through his job before the darkness hit him, both from the fading sky and his parched mouth. Today was a brand new day. Today, he'd finish the job, but he'd need some tools first. Good thing he didn't actually sell his jigsaw in the pawn shop. He needed it after all.

Making his way back to his pickup, his ears picked up the buzz of chattering voices. Two women in fluorescent headbands and knee length neon socks were power-walking straight to him to the tune of their gossip.

One with long, straight brown hair, and the other with — *gulp* — curly blonde.

"Can you believe it? This makes the third one in a few weeks. It's getting scary." The brunette huffed her sentences out to the tempo of her feet.

"So I heard. All blondes, too, right?" her friend answered.

She looked like an older version of Pigtails from yesterday. She had the same color hair, the same straight back, and the same wrinkle in her forehead that proved she was thinking harder than she needed to be. The woman even had the same wide eyes, as if she were taking in every detail around her. Richard's hands began to sweat. This was definitely the mother that may or may not have been watching him, according to Pigtails herself.

"That's what I hear."

"Think you could help me dye mine, then? I'd feel much safer if I didn't look like … you know ... all those other women."

"You don't. You don't look like any of them. You look like you. You don't have to change yourself because there's some creep wandering around here."

Richard could almost hear the brunette roll her eyes.

"That's easy for you to say."

The two women slowed their pace as they approached Richard at his truck. Both of them addressed him with narrowed eyes. He waved, giving them a quiet smile and hoping they would continue past. He knew he didn't belong there. Not really. He didn't know what he would say if they had any questions.

The brunette moved toward Richard's right shoulder, and standing on either side of him, they both power-walked in place. Their feet drummed on the pavement like a quickened *tick-tick-tick* of a counting down clock.

"Good morning," the brunette said through her heavy breath.

"Morning." Richard mustered up his best morning cheer.

The blonde on his left mumbled a, "Hi," as she popped a hair tie off her wrist and fixed her hair on the top of her head, hiding its texture. Blonde curls, just like Amy. Just like Alisha. Just like Michelle and Leslie and his own mother. *Momma.* She had slid into a spot with the parade of dead women on every news station.

"You working on the house?" The brunette cocked an eyebrow.

Crap. They did have questions. "Hm?" Richard noticed her gaze behind him. His pile of boards on display. "Oh, yeah. Um, you could say that."

The blonde slowed down her in-place jog. "I don't know if there's anything that can be done to that house that would make anyone want to buy it." Her voice sounded shaky, like she might as well have been talking about a ghost instead of a building.

Richard swung his eyes her way. "That house? It's in great shape. Got good bones on it and everything. There's even a brand new back porch. That alone will add some value to it." He felt slightly embarrassed for getting defensive about a house he never stepped foot in, let alone owned — the house that might actually own his tree.

"I don't think he knows." Brunette's feet slowed down their rhythmic thud-thud-thud. Clearly this woman was one for small talk and gossip. Gladys would like her.

"What don't I know?"

"I guess he doesn't."

The two women were giving him whiplash talking on both sides of him.

"About what happened there just earlier this week. Jennifer Graves lived in the house. She was such a pretty little thing. A really great neighbor, too. She had that porch built just a few weeks ago. She said there were a couple of house projects that needed to get done, but if she could keep up with the gardening, then at least she was doing something to keep the house up."

Richard's palms moistened at the choice in wording. "Was?"

"Um-hm. She had these beautiful golden curls that made us all jealous. They reminded me of that woman I saw on the news … what was her name? You know, the one with the pigs."

"Michelle," the blonde woman squeaked out. She noticeably fidgeted with her own hair, trying to flatten out anything that might have been poking out of her freshly made ponytail.

"That's right; Michelle. Anyway, Jennifer was quiet, kept to herself mostly. But it was always great to see her watering her front gardens while out on a run. She'd smile and wave, ask us how we were doing, then get back to making her garden beautiful. We always saw her when we got out for our little jogs, didn't we?"

Ponytail nodded her head as her cheeks flushed. Richard didn't think it was from her in-place power walk.

"Then just a few days ago, she wasn't in her front yard to wave at us. Turns out, someone broke in and killed her. Can you believe that?"

All the moisture in Richard's mouth disappeared. The butterflies were dried out, too, and he wished he were rummaging through his box by the oak tree instead of standing sandwiched between two women whose feet continued to dance in place.

"And just like that, she wasn't there any more. They were quick to clean up, too. Within a single day, they poked around the scene and hired a company to scrub the floors clean. And since it was a rental property, the sale sign popped up almost immediately. I guess the owners didn't want to keep it around if it's known as the murder house. I can't say I blame them. I wouldn't want to own it either." She took a quick pause and shook her head. "It's like nothing of Jennifer exists there anymore. Nothing but her memory, really. Whatever was left of that."

He snuck another gaze at the house. This perfectly manicured house was a hollow shell left behind by a woman whose face was probably splattered across social media by now, adding to the parade of pretty blonde women.

One more gone.

The only life left on this property was the oak tree. Her leaves rustled through a breeze, calling him back, begging him to finish the work he started.

"Work," it whispered to him. *"Home."*

"Come on. We should go."

Richard turned around to see Ponytail now forcibly holding her friend's elbow, guiding her away. He wasn't sure exactly, but thought he could hear distrust in her voice. He didn't blame her. He didn't even trust himself.

Brunette shrugged her off. "I told you, you have nothing to worry about. But if you insist, I'll help you color it later. I think I have another box of dye from the last time I treated my own hair." Gesturing to Richard, she gave a polite, "See you around. Good luck with the renovations!"

Richard was finally able to get into his truck. He shoved his hand under the seats and found his jigsaw. The tangled cord of his phone charger was wrapped around it, like a vine choking out the posts of a fence. Perfect. It was funny how he unintentionally kept the one thing that would be incredibly useful to him. To *her*. And now, he could use it to escalate to the next phase of building.

Was *he* escalating?

A tiny *clink* sounded from beneath the seat when he pulled it out, so he stuck his hand under again and fished out a lone bottle. His favorite bourbon.

Miracles do happen.

It probably fell out from his box, but he gladly accepted the tiny miracle that he could taste his drink now, before he got back to work.

"Come home," the whisper called him again.

It was clear she would let him rest when he was done and not a moment before.

With his saw in hand, he went to work on his claimed wood, cutting in all the places he measured the night before. He ignored the splinters that punctured his skin and blew the dust clouds from obstructing his sight. His experience allowed him to work with ease, but his desire helped him work with care. He wasn't just building a treehouse. He was building a home under the stars that would keep his hands away from Amy. He did belong here, after all.

"I'll take care of you, Amy. I promised I'd do better, and I'm going to keep my word. I'll do better for you. For me. For us."

Amy. He didn't mean to call the tree by the name, but it slipped out. The butterflies must have named her.

With only a couple of boards left to cut, Richard's saw battery puttered to a stop. He scratched his neck and looked up to the sky, letting the Vitamin D cover his face, trying to figure out what to do next. "Sorry, Amy." He let out a sigh. "That's the best I can do."

"Keep going," the whisper told him. *"Keep. Going."*

He shook his head. "If there's no battery, I can't."

"Keep ... going." A small gust of wind blew some of the leaves up from the ground. He watched them dance in the air and flutter back toward him, almost pushing themselves on his chest, causing him to step backwards.

As they fell back to the ground, he inhaled and breathed in clarity. The house. Not his house, but the empty house. Maybe it still had electricity. Maybe Jennifer had to go so he could use the electricity without anyone questioning. Maybe…

No. He shouldn't have been happy about that. She was a woman. A person. Kind and beautiful according to the jogging women. Her death wasn't a good thing. But if her electricity was still on, that would be very helpful. He could be happy about that.

He walked past the balding grass where the lumber pile had sat and crept further up. It felt both intrusive and electrifying being so close to a home he didn't belong in. No one was there to 'catch' him in mid-act. And even if they did, he now had a cover story. He was just another one of the contractors, fixing up a sad house for a new family to move in. If the two jogging women would believe it, then so would the rest of the neighborhood.

"I'll be home soon." He assumed his own whisper would carry over to the tree, to *her*.

He found the silver outlet near the freshly constructed deck. He flipped the cover up and hoped for the best. With eyes closed, he eased the battery plug into the socket. A perfect, snug fit.

A tiny beep called for his eyes to open. There *was* electricity — another sign he was exactly where he was supposed to be.

Thank you, Jennifer.

He sunk to the ground and sat with his back against the siding. His tree looked so small from here. *She* looked so small. If he didn't know any better, he would think his eyes were playing tricks on him. But he did know better. The oak looked that way because it wasn't a part of this house. It was its own entity, not tied to ownership to anyone but him.

As long as *she* would have him, he would have *her*.

Just then, a *ding* rang from his pocket. His phone.

The battery must be dying in my phone, too.

Sure enough, the notification at the top told him it needed a charge. Before he attached it to the house to siphon off electricity as well, he unlocked the screen. He just wanted to see — just check.

The corners of his mouth tugged when he found Amy's profile. Her profile picture smiled back at him. Those green eyes with golden flecks … he swore no one had eyes like those.

The sound of leaves falling from his tree reminded him that she, too, wore multiple colors on display.

"I see you," he called out to *her*.

The Amy on his phone kept her smile. He wished he could speak to her now. Not that he ever could hold a conversation with her very well in person before. But his imagination conjured up a scenario where he could talk to her without shying away, fumbling over his words, or wanting to throw her against the wall and explore every inch of her to see if it matched up to his fantasies.

"How are you doing, Amelia?"

She smiled.

"I'm sorry, Amy. I know you keep having to remind me to call you that." He rubbed the back of his neck. "How are you doing, Amy?"

She smiled.

The tree whispered, "*Cold.*"

Richard shrugged it off. "I miss you, you know. Out here, away from Bridgewell. It's strange not seeing you on the front steps, smiling at everyone walking by. I think you were the only good thing that place ever saw."

"*I'm cold*," the whisper came again.

"I wish I could have told you that in person. It just — it never felt right. You have Neil. The two of you are like … are like … I don't know. Like bourbon and Coke, I guess." He chuckled at the inappropriate simile. "Or, like peas and carrots. Or peanut butter and jelly. Like … oranges and sunshine. My point is, the two of you have always belonged together. I know that. I'm okay with that. You do so much good together, and everyone knows it. Everyone sees it and feels it and, well, I guess I just wish I were good enough to be that good, too. I wish I were enough, Amy. I promise I'll do better. It's kind of why I'm here, you know? For you. To do better for you."

"*So cold.*"

Richard was getting annoyed at the whispering tree from Whispering Pass. He wanted to keep a conversation with this Amy, the one that smiled back at him.

"I saw you were going to a health convention, weren't you? I bet you enjoyed that — talking to people about nuts and vitamins or whatever it is all the people who know what they're doing talk about." Richard hoped the change of topic would make the whispering stop, but it didn't.

It kept taunting him, "Cold…"

He ignored it. "I bet you'll come back with a new brilliant piece of advice for Gladys. She won't appreciate it, but it'll be good for you to give it to her anyway. She doesn't realize it, but she needs someone to look after her. We all do."

He let his thumb scroll through the feed. He wanted her to tell him the types of things she did at the convention. He wanted to hear all about the people she met and the new tips she wanted to share. "Let's see…" But the only photos that showed up were the same ones from before. No updates. No selfies with her coworkers. No new volunteer status … no new content at all. Nothing was new in Amy's life that he didn't already know.

He frowned. "Don't you want to tell me what you did? I'd love to hear it." But no amount of scrolling gave him any new information.

Why is there nothing? Nothing at all?

"Don't you want to talk about it?"

Why hasn't she updated?

"Isn't there anything you want to tell me about?"

Another beep. His saw was charged. As he switched cords, he tried to convince himself that Amy had her reasons for keeping secrets. She was allowed to be quiet once in a while. Amy Jones didn't have to report to Richard or anyone else. Except maybe Neil.

He squeezed his hands together, squishing the invisible sticky substance between them.

He didn't have to like it. He wasn't in any position to care one way or the other, no matter what the butterflies told him. Besides, he couldn't let the Amy on his phone distract him from the Amy he was meant to have. With a full battery on his jigsaw, he could now make his final cuts. He left the phone there to charge and he was on his way back to the tree, his pocket tinging with the sound of loose nails.

"I'm cold."

"I'm coming, Amy. It won't take much longer. I'm just about done."

As the minutes ticked by, Richard finished the final cuts and began piecing together the wooden pieces into a larger-than-life puzzle. Boards nestled snugly between the branches. They fell into place, creating a platform his large body could spread out on. Each piece of lumber snapped into place around him as if they had always belonged there. And when he was done, he realized they did. Sitting with four walls he built with his own hands, he realized this was where he belonged, too — unattached to someone else's form of home and in a place that felt strong, protective, and comfortable.

"We're home, Amy. You don't have to be cold anymore."

Exhausted from his labor, Richard splayed out in his new home, letting the vitamin D — the sunshine he could have — peek through the tiny spaces between the boards and soak into his skin. He didn't even notice his stomach growl or his parched lips ask for a taste of bourbon. He had found where he belonged, and it was right here. Right with *her*.

CHAPTER EIGHTEEN

"I've got it, Mom, I've got it!"

Mills pinched together the helmet straps under her chin. She didn't know why her mom insisted on helping her every time. She wasn't a little kid anymore and had probably put on her own helmet a billion times. Especially at night. By herself. In the dark. Though, she would never tell her mom that. There would never be an end to the fit over her roaming around after bedtime by herself.

Grown-ups were so silly. They always told you not to throw a fit, but they'd throw one at the drop of a hat if they knew you weren't following one silly rule they made up just for you.

"Come back home in thirty minutes, Mills. You hear me?" Her mom fiddled with her hair, tucking it behind her ear. Hiding it from plain sight.

"Loud and clear, Mom. I'm just going to skate down the block a little and come back home."

"Straight home. Don't talk to strangers." She bit her bottom lip. "I don't like sending you out on your own like this."

"Then why do you?" Mills scrunched up her face and threw a hand on her hip. "If you don't like it, don't do it." The logic was reasonable to her. If she didn't like cleaning her room, she just didn't. No reason to do something you didn't like if it bugged you that much. Well, unless you were threatened with no dessert or a grounding. Then you sucked it up and did it, whether you liked it or not. No one liked missing out on cupcakes if they were available.

"Because Mrs. Beasley is right. You need to be able to play without your mother hovering over your shoulder every second of the day."

Mills rolled her eyes. "And you do everything that Mrs. Beasley tells you to?"

"Of course not, love." Her mom straightened her stance. "Besides, you go way too fast on that board of yours. You know my old knees can't keep up with you."

Mills grabbed her board and opened up the front door for herself. "Well then, I guess you and Mrs. Beasley need to speed up your walks, huh? You're not that old. You could practice a little so you can get faster and catch up to my speed."

Mom sighed while Mills walked out the door. "Just be careful, please. Love you!"

"Back atcha!"

With that, Mills was on her board and rolling down the street. Daytime strolling wasn't nearly as interesting as the night time adventures, but it gave her a reason to be out in the sunshine instead of cooped up in the house. And that was good enough for her.

Down the road, off of Beacon, she slowed her roll. That white truck was still parked there, in front of *that* house. And that man was still there, too.

Weird.

She dropped her foot to the ground to stop her movement. What was that man doing?

He had big pieces of wood propped up by that tree that looked like an old man's face. Only, the tree didn't look the same as it always had. Some of the wood pieces were nailed into the tree, like a box. It made the tree far less scary and a little more interesting.

She watched him use a little saw to cut another piece and nail it to what was already there. The little box was filling up, and she realized he was building a treehouse.

The funny-smelling man was building a treehouse!

Now, this was exciting news. There were a few kids in the neighborhood who would play in the branches of that old-man tree during the summers. They had each asked their parents if they could build a house in it. Their argument was if this was a place where kids could play, then why not make it a more fun place to play? It would be better than wandering around in the middle of the street playing chicken with the cars or ding dong ditch to see how much faster they were than the old people answering their doors.

None of the grown-ups saw it that way. They said it was a "common area," whatever that meant, but since it wasn't on their property, they couldn't build whatever they wanted on it. They were putting their foot down on another stupid, silly rule.

The grown-ups probably didn't want to put in the effort of building anything on it. Figures. They were always making excuses not to do something fun.

She sat down on the side of the road, in front of the truck to watch. This man was cutting the wood pieces left and right. One by one, he'd put another piece up until there was a wall. It was fascinating to watch, as if this man knew what every grown-up in Whispering Pass had said no to and decided he would say yes instead. He was either crazy or brilliant, and she wanted to know which it was.

Before long, her stomach growled. She should have packed a snack. An orange sounded good. Sweet, juicy, refreshing. But what about this man? Even a little bit of skateboarding made her feel hungry. She could only imagine how hungry this man should have been building a whole house.

Well, a treehouse. But it was still a pretty cool-looking house.

But since he never stopped to eat — what would he have to eat out here anyway? — she didn't either.

Who was this man? He showed up out of nowhere, and now he was building something all the kids had wanted. Grown-ups didn't do that kind of thing, not without having a secret attached to it.

What was this man's secret? She couldn't tell. Secrets weren't something grown-ups allowed out in the open, during daylight. She kicked one of the leaves that landed by her foot. It was so frustrating that she couldn't tell why this man was here. It didn't seem right, but it also didn't seem completely wrong either.

The man walked away from the tree and over to *that* house. He bent over to touch something, maybe pick something up, but she couldn't tell what. He slid down and sat on the ground.

She felt the ground under her. It was cold. She imagined he was probably cold, too. That made her feel sorry for him. Grown-ups weren't supposed to be out in the cold like that. They weren't like kids. Kids didn't care if they were cold and uncomfortable as long as they were having fun. But grown-ups? They'd rather be inside and out of the cold if they could.

Maybe this was a different kind of grown-up. Maybe he was having fun?

That wasn't it. He didn't look like he was having fun. He looked like he was on a mission. She thought about the creeper man who spider-crawled into the house. He was on a mission, too.

She squinted her eyes at the man sitting on the ground behind the house. Maybe some secret-keepers hid their secrets out in the open. Had she been wrong all along? Were some secrets so obvious she could figure them out before everyone else fell asleep? Would daytime be just as good to snoop around and see what's going on?

Maybe it was.

She looked at the tree. It really wasn't as scary as it used to be. This thing in front of her looked like it could be a pretty good fort if she were allowed in it. If the other kids saw this, they'd freak out. They'd be all over that little almost-made room, fighting over who should stake their claim on it.

But something told her, no one would be able to claim it. Not with this guy around. She felt like this guy needed this tree house for some reason. She just couldn't figure it out yet. A breeze rushed by and pulled some of the leaves off the tree's branches, and it almost sounded like it was talking to her.

That was dumb. Trees don't talk.

She strained her ears anyway. What would a tree have to say if it could, though? Would it tell her any of the hidden secrets? Probably not.

She huffed out a sigh as she bent her neck to face the sky. Being an inquisitive kid was hard work. She could be out here all day and still not know everything that was going on.

All day. Crap. She had been out nearly all day.

At least, longer than thirty minutes. Her mom was going to kill her.

Well, maybe not kill. But she was definitely going to put on her worry face and ask a million questions like where she had been and if she talked to any strangers. At least she could be honest about that one. She hadn't talked to anybody at all. Not this time anyway.

She slammed the board down on its wheels and pushed her foot forward. Her stomach growled as she made her way down Beacon Street all the way home. Maybe her mom would take pity on her empty stomach and worry about that more than anything else.

For now, Mills had to keep a long list of questions to find the answers to and a log of the things she was keeping an eye on for herself. One day, things were going to break wide open, and she would need to use the answers that came with it.

Maybe she'd bring an offering to him tomorrow. Maybe an orange. It'd be just the right ice breaker to see if he was the suspicious kind of person to look for or not.

CHAPTER NINETEEN

Tick. Tick. Tick. Richard's drowsy eyes opened to inspect the tiny repetitive noise pulling him out of sleep. Surprisingly, he didn't have a headache. His body was sore, but this was a welcome ache from his normal annoying hangovers

No. He didn't pass out. He just fell asleep.

He fell asleep and woke up in the same place twice in a row. This he could get used to. This was the feeling of home. This meant Amy would stay safe.

Thank the freaking sunshine.

But there was an annoying dig in the back of his mind. Yesterday, Amy hadn't told him anything. Not tree-Amy, but phone-Amy. No social media. No updates. Just a blank smile that meant nothing. *She would stay safe, wouldn't she?*

Tick tick tick.

There it was again. He pulled himself off the floor and stepped to the open door frame.

A familiar form stood outside, picking up fallen acorns and tossing them up. Each one hit against the treehouse wall with another *tick.*

Pigtails.

"Hey, what's the big idea?" He rubbed the confusion from his eyes, then sat down with his legs dangling from the open frame of his treehouse. He screwed up his face in curiosity. Why this little girl was trying to get his attention was beyond him.

"So you really are up there, mister." She spat on the ground. "Thought you might be."

"Is that so?" Richard crossed his arms. She had been watching him. Just like she had promised.

"Told you I was keeping an eye out on you."

A nod and a chuckle. "So you did." She really was the opposite of her paranoid mother.

Pigtails rubbed the sole of her foot in the dirt and dried leaves. The sound of mid-autumn crunched beneath her feet. "I brought you somethin'." She looked like she was somewhere between wanting to offer a gift and wanting to keep her distance. Proof she was a smart kid to be so unsure.

He was unsure of himself, too.

Confused, Richard dug his pinky in his ear. "I must be hearing things. I thought you said you brought me something."

"I *did* say I brought you somethin'." Another spit on the ground. When she appeared satisfied it hit the ground in a *splat*, Pigtails slipped her black backpack off her shoulder and sat it on top of the gathering leaves. She unzipped the top and reached in.

Within a moment, she pulled out her fist and yelled, "Catch!"

So she did have a gift.

Instinctively, Richard threw his hand up and like a catcher's mitt, caught something round and cold. His own reflexes took him by surprise. "An orange?"

She pulled out a second orange from her pack and helped herself to peeling it. "Yup. My momma said that they're good for you. They help give you energy and keep your system healthy." She flicked a piece of peel to the ground. "Or, somethin' like that." She shrugged. "All I know is that they're sweet and juicy. And sometimes after a long day, I know I need somethin' that will give me energy. I figured you might need it, too."

Richard knitted his brow. This was some curious kid.

The smell of new orange hit him hard with the memory of a package on his doorstep.

The oranges from Amy. The oranges she left for him the day he walked away from his mother's body. He let himself slide into the memory.

The first taste didn't even taste like fruit. It tasted like detachment.

He didn't realize he had paused his movement in mid peel until she jolted him out of memory.

"Don't eat it if you don't want to." She flung another piece of peel on the ground. "But I figured you might want somethin' since you're camping out in a tree like a weirdo."

She wasn't wrong. He did want something. And oranges and vitamin D or C or whatever sounded like a pretty good something to have. Richard dug his thumb to pull back the peel. This time, the fresh scent filled him with comfort. The little piece of protection in his hands made him wish he could share the moment with Amy. The real Amy. But the further away he was from her, the more he could keep her protected. He leaned his weight against his tree. The tree Amy would have to do.

"Thanks, Pigtails."

"That ain't my name, you know." She cocked her head to the side and squinted her eyes. "So, why are you camping up there like that? It seems…"

"Weird?" He used her own word back at her.

She nodded in agreement. "Yeah, that."

Richard glanced around him, eyeing the sunlight between boards in his makeshift home. At about the size of a small bedroom, he had enough room to lay out his full length as long as he didn't stretch his body too much. The corner of his room held his box of spare clothes and airplane bottles — the only closet he needed. The whole sight probably did look a little strange. This was where little kids should climb and play, but it looked more like the world's most unfortunate man cave.

The butterflies sent ripples of goosebumps down his arms. He crossed his arms to calm the prickling feeling.

"What makes you think I'm camping here?"

Pigtails threw her pack on her back and squinted up at him. "Pretty obvious, isn't it? This treehouse wasn't here before. Sure, it was somethin' some of the kids talked about begging their parents for, but it never happened. None of the grown-ups ever wanted to build one. Then you showed up and threw one up overnight. I thought maybe one of the grown-ups had asked you to build it, but your truck has been parked on the street ever since, collecting dust, as my momma calls it."

Momma. Sticky hands. Red sauce.

"She says it's not normal that a contractor hasn't moved from this spot. That there must be some bigger things to do in *that* house than she realized." The girl pursed her lips as she hitched her temple. "That's what she calls it, you know. *That* house. Says to keep an eye out for suspicious strangers and not to talk to nobody I don't know." She kept her eyes locked on Richard's as she scratched the top of her head. "The police said the same thing, too."

And now the police were involved?

"So … why are you talking to me, then? Aren't I a stranger?" His sweat piled in his palms, and it made them feel even more covered in the non-existent sauce.

"You ain't a suspicious one. You're just a weird one. And weird isn't somethin' to be afraid of. Weird isn't what got the lady that lived in *that* house."

"I see," but Richard wasn't so sure. His blackouts and wakeups were too coincidentally matching up to the parade of blonde women all over the news.

"So, why are you camping out there?" Pigtails asked again. Clearly, she expected an answer and wasn't going to leave empty-handed.

"That's a good question, kid." Richard shuffled his feet over the edge of his treehouse. "I suppose it's just where I need to be right now."

"Aint you got anywhere else to be?"

Richard's eyes mimicked the same thoughtful expression the girl gave him a minute ago.

No, he didn't. This was the only place for him. The only place where he felt a connection. The only place where he felt safe. So that Amy could be safe. Safe and…

"*Cold,*" the whisper interrupted his thoughts.

His eyes widened, and the butterflies crawled through his spine. The whisper never showed up around other people before. He wondered if Pigtails could hear it, too.

"Guess you don't. That's strange, too, you know."

"You got me there, kid. It sure is."

She shuffled her feet on the ground, making a small dirt trail within the fallen leaves. "Sometimes it gets cold, you know."

Richard nodded. "So I've heard."

"*I'm cold*," the whisper repeated. Could she hear it, too?

"How you gonna keep yourself from freezing when it gets colder?"

The cold. It had crept up on him, following him from the moment he felt his mother's cold touch. The cold shoulder he regretfully gave Amy, the cold autumn wind that blew in seemingly overnight, the cold response to leaving Amy at the food drive. The cold look Neil shot him while sitting on his couch.

The cold began in his fingertips, crawled up his arms, and seeped into the pit of his stomach where the butterflies cycled through it, absorbing the cold, spitting it out, and taking it back in over and over everywhere Richard moved.

He had been trying to warm the chill with golden liquid and remorse. But no amount of bottles he tipped back would keep the cold out.

"*I'm cold*." The whisper's relentless reminder told him that this was his responsibility. He had brought the cold here, to this tree. And now he needed to fix it, to protect *her*.

The breeze picked up around him, pulling more leaves out of the oak's branches. It was almost like she was giving him an offering, a solution she couldn't carry out on her own. The leaves. They'd keep him and *her* warm.

"I've got an idea. Think you might want to help?"

She shrugged her shoulders. "Depends on what that idea is, I guess."

"Well, how crafty are you, kid?"

She gave a soft scoff as she wrinkled her nose. "What, you got some glitter and sequins in your tree, mister? I'm more of a dirt and mud kind of girl. I don't have time for cut and paste projects."

Richard flung his body from the treehouse, his feet landing with a *swish* of the leaves under his feet. "Good. That's just the kind of crafty I need." He pulled his keys from his pocket and gestured to his truck on the side of the road. "I'm not much for cut and paste either. However, I've got something in my truck over there—"

"Ut uh. I ain't going anywhere near your old, child-snatching truck, mister."

He was starting to like this kid. "You're right, kid. You're smart. You shouldn't. I tell you what, though, if you stay right here, I'll go grab what I need and come back. If you don't have anything better to do, you can hang around and help me with a dirt and mud kind of craft. Of course, you don't have to if you don't want to. I wouldn't want your momma to think you're hanging around anyone suspicious."

"I told you. You're weird, not suspicious."

Richard chuckled under his breath. He liked her spunk and honesty. He imagined this was how Gladys Nightingale might have been as a kid. Unabashed with keen eyes on the happenings around her. Only this kid would never age to a rocking stoop on her front porch. She'd end up doing something big and important, to keep 'suspicious' at bay.

When he opened his truck door, a stale alcohol scent wafted out into the open. He couldn't remember the last time that smell made him choke instead of pine for a fresh sip.

Ha. Maybe I really am doing better, Amy.

After waving the air out of his truck, he leaned in and scooped his hand on the floorboards, grabbing a handful of plastic bags from truck stops and fast food joints. Hundreds of yellow smiley faces stared back in their painted expressions. He cradled them in his arms, then made a second and third sweep until the floorboards showed themselves for the first time in months. It felt strange to realize he forgot the color of his floorboards until now. Gray. They were gray. Imagine that.

Pigtails kicked at the ground again, rubbing at it with the toes of her shoes. "Whatcha gonna do with that trash there, mister?"

Richard thrust over a handful of bags to her. "It's how I'm going to keep out the cold."

He pulled one open by the handles and scooped up a fist full of gold and brown oak leaves, shoving them inside until it looked like an overstuffed pillow complete with a yellow smiley face on the front. Satisfied with a round and bulging bag, he tied the handles together, creating two little ears in a knot on top. With a heave, he tossed it up and over and into the treehouse opening. It landed there with a soft thud.

"Tada!"

Pigtails chuckled. "You really are crazy, mister."

Even so, she opened her bags and, one by one, filled them to the top until they were nearly bursting. With each finished bag, she tossed it to

Richard so he could, in turn, toss it into his humble abode. They worked like this, in a tiny assembly line, with only the sound of crunching leaves ticking the time away.

There was no need for conversation. What would he talk to a nine-year-old about anyway? Talking about cartoons or candy or whatever it was that kids were interested in would only keep them from their work, and he had to keep the cold at bay. The whisper would never let him get away without addressing it. He took a glance at Pigtails as she finished tying another bag. This wasn't a cartoon and candy type of kid, anyway.

When her arms were free of all the bags, Pigtails brushed the leaf crumbs off her pants. "Well, that was interesting."

"Not weird?"

She scrunched up her mouth, acting as if she was going to spit on the ground, but she stopped herself before she did.

"No. It was *interesting.*"

She adjusted her bag on her shoulders and stepped back to look at the treehouse, it's doorless door frame now full with a pile of leaf-bags. Some brown. Some green. Some with leaves that looked like golden flecks. All of it, just carcasses of nature.

She hesitated, sucking in a deep breath. "I think maybe there's somethin' I need to ask you."

Richard noticed her eyes gloss over. She wasn't looking at him anymore. She was looking through him and right at the tree. Right at *her*.

"What's that, kid?"

"Can you breathe, diddle diddle?"

CHAPTER TWENTY

Richard's knees fell to the floor with a dry slam. His muscles shook uncontrollably as the walls spun around him in spiraled shapes. His palms pressed down on the bowed wooden floor underneath him, trying desperately to keep himself from knocking the consciousness out of memory. He could feel a hundred smiling plastic bags burning holes into him with their glassy vacant eyes.

His body wanted to feed itself alcohol. His mind wanted to feed itself closure.

His sticky hands and phone-Amy's smile kept a wound in his heart wide open.

Richard left Bridgewell Apartments to keep the real Amy safe, but if there was no proof, no update, no nothing of her at all…

Why hasn't she shared anything? Nothing at all?

When he had tacked the bags on the wall, he hadn't focused on the faces. His entire concentration was on their purpose. He had been so focused on keeping out the cold, the bags blurred together as a giant leafy mass.

But something inside Richard shattered the moment he finished tacking the last bag up. When he took in the sight around him, he noticed all those blank yellow faces. They surrounded him from every side with little unhinged smiles and unblinking expressions. If their mouths could move, they'd laugh in uncomfortable snickers. But they stayed gaping open.

And the smell from earlier had deepened. The rotting, dead smell close by. Wherever it was coming from, it had crawled out up and around his tree, pulling every branch into a bubble of putrid gas. He took another look at those open yellow mouths and his imagination filled in the blanks — bad breath.

No. That didn't make sense either.

Where was Amy? Was she okay? Why couldn't his mind break itself from thinking about another man's wife? He was so thirsty.

His eyes shut in tight locks to block out the yellow faces gawking at him, asking him to go check on his former neighbor. See how okay she really was.

He gasped for breath, filling his lungs in short bursts of painful oxygen. On tightened hands and knees, he crawled to the corner of his little room, hoping for something that would loosen him up.

His fingertips bumped his cardboard box. With a grateful slice of hope, he reached over the side and grabbed the first glass bottle his fingers found. In a single motion, he ripped open the cap and shoved the opening to his mouth.

Even with heaving gulps, he couldn't drink it fast enough. His addiction craved relief, and he wanted to oblige. It was the only thing that could numb him from the panic attack rising from his chest.

The faces paraded around him in their yellow hues, just like the shades of blonde worn by all the women on parade themselves.

Why was he still thinking of Amy?

The bottle was now empty. Not even enough to trickle down the sides as he tipped it upside down. His taste buds had already forgotten the flavor of the last drop. He frowned. He had hoped downing the entire drink would have stopped his head from spinning in wide loops.

It didn't.

It made them worse. The circling flies didn't help either.

Bzzz.

Another bottle found its way in his hands.

He tipped that one back, too.

The house, *the* house, by the tree showed itself through the door frame opening. Richard's eyes did their best to fix themselves on it.

Bzzz.

With another unbalanced step, he eased himself down to a sitting position. His legs dangled over the side like an overgrown child in his fort. Maybe this view could keep the crawling anxiety at bay.

He tried to force himself to see the non-existent woman who didn't live there anymore.

Jennifer. Maybe if he thought about Jennifer, he could stop himself from obsessing over Amy.

Bzzz. Bzzz.

There was a window, two actually. They looked easy enough to access. All it would take is a push or two, and maybe the guts to hoist himself into a stranger's house. He imagined creeping up to one of the windows and bringing his hands up to it to feel the cold glass under his palms.

Bzzz.

What would he have done after he got himself through the window?

Find the woman living there?

Would he talk to her?

Creep from behind her?

Would he whisper to her or sing a song in her ear?

Would he threaten her with his hands? With a tool? With a knife? His saw?

Bzzz.

But it really didn't matter what imaginary thing he would do once he imagined himself in there, because it all ended the same, didn't it? It all ended with another dead woman whose last breath was forcefully taken from her sooner than natural fate would have allowed.

Bzzz. Bzzz. Bzzz.

He imagined standing in the house's hallway, a lady's body splayed out on the floor in front of him. Her limbs starfished out just like his momma. Her hair haloed around her in tendrils that would never be twisted around her fingers again. Her eyes glossed over, unblinking, forever in a state of searching for the man responsible, the Samhale Strangler.

She would never find him. She'd never have the chance to.

Blonde curls, wispy tendrils, unblinking eyes.

Where. Was. Amy?

Bzzzzzzzz.

He couldn't breathe, and when he tried, he sucked in stale air that gagged him. Whatever had died nearby filled his closing nostrils.

His eyes closed again and he tipped back the bottle in his hands until it was as empty as the first. The image behind his eyelids stayed tattooed to the spot. The blonde woman on the floor, waiting for an answer. He crept toward her, wanting to hold her. Wanting to do something to her...for her. He wanted to turn back time and make whatever happened to her never happen in the first place.

But then he looked at her face and it wasn't hers anymore.

Amy. It was Amy's face.

"Amy," his voice broke as he said her name out loud.

The blonde ringlets framed her cherub face, drawing his eyes to hers. The little golden flecks weren't there anymore. They had disappeared in her lifeless stare.

He had never gotten close to hugging her at the apartment. Never would have even tried. But here, in his thoughts, he wanted to hold her tight. This was a new ache he needed to satisfy. He felt if he didn't pull her close to his body, he would lose her forever. She'd fade from existence itself completely.

His shaking hands creeped slowly to her, afraid the slightest touch might harm the body in front of him. In his thought-world, he scooped his hand under her head to cradle it on his lap.

In the treehouse, he scooped his hand under one of the untacked bags and laid it over his thighs.

His other hand brushed the golden tendrils out of her face, rubbing her paling cheek.

His thumb was over the yellow smiling face, caressing the plastic film as a fly landed on the bag's eye.

He took her hand into his and interlocked fingers with her, exhaling with relief that he finally knew what her hands felt like.

On the treehouse floor, dried leaves crumpled in his hands, falling into dust between his digits.

Something moved in his hand, and he swore Amy was tugging back at his fingers.

He let out a whimpered, "Amy," and tried to grasp onto her hold tighter.

He never wanted to open his eyes. He never wanted to let go. He had *her* here, now.

Then, the whisper was back. It came from the stink in Amy's mouth. *"I'm cold,"* it said. And he knew plastic bag insulation wasn't going to be enough to keep the cold at bay.

CHAPTER TWENTY-ONE

Richard blinked. He didn't remember pulling apart the leaf-bags in his tree-home. Nor did he remember finishing the second bottle of liquor and starting a third.

He didn't remember brushing away the accumulating flies buzzing in and out of the tree hollow.

He didn't remember starting up his truck, tucking that third bottle into the passenger's seat like a maltreated child.

He definitely didn't remember how he got where he was now: experiencing *déjà vu* in his parking space, watching Gladys Nightingale rock on her porch chair with a cigarette dangling from her mouth.

That's right. It was for Amy. He had to see Amy.

With the parade of women growing larger, he had to see for himself that she wasn't joining them. His mind wouldn't let it go. His fists wouldn't either.

"Well, hello, Richard. Not done gracing us with your presence are you?" Gladys stared him down, with eyes that begged for the story of where Richard had been.

"Where is she?" The butterflies forced Richard's heartbeat to quicken at the possible answer. "Where's Amy?" His heart prayed Gladys kept her eyes on Amy enough to pinpoint her safety right now. At this moment.

Please, Gladys. Your nosy self should be good for something.

"Amelia?" Gladys threw her thumb over her shoulder. "Amelia Jones? If she ain't home, she's probably at work or volunteering at the soup kitchen or visiting sick old folks in their homes or something. I can't keep track of that woman. She's all over the place fussing over anyone she gets a hold of; she could be anywhere." She cocked an eyebrow up while she sucked in a taste of nicotine.

Flashes of Amy's volunteer photos filled Richard's thoughts. Photos of her at the soup kitchen, in front of the library, in a crowd of people wearing Habitat for Humanity T-shirts.

And yet, her social media didn't show anything new in the past few days. No new volunteer status, helping hand update, or shared selfie. Social media said she wasn't around.

But the thing that was around? Pictures of the dead women who resembled Amy. Beautiful soldiers who marched to the beat of serving others who were all corpses left by someone's hands.

Whose freaking hands?

Chills covered his spine. He didn't want to compare Amy's picture to theirs. If he did, that would mean...

"Where. Is. She?" Richard's words came out like punches in the air. His eyes darted between number 76 and Gladys's expression. Her eyes didn't move from their widened stance.

"I don't know. I guess—I guess it's been a while. She's a busy girl, you know that."

"Yeah, busy." He wasn't convinced. Again, there was no social media proof she ever made it to that health conference. No word. No photo. Nothing.

Richard stomped his feet down the sidewalk. He didn't mean to throw a tantrum, but his feet felt heavy. *He* felt heavy. His side ached at the memory of hitting the railing on the Joneses' front porch. If she wasn't standing behind door 76, then he'd have even darker monsters to face within himself. Darker than his alcoholic demons. Darker than anything he could drown out or choke down.

The same red car was parked in front of number 76. His insides turned to thick sludge that the butterflies couldn't move through.

Richard didn't even bother looking inside it. He knew no one was behind the wheel. Either he had been too oblivious or whoever owned that car had been elusive from the moment it first showed up. It didn't matter at the moment. The only thing that mattered was Amy.

Richard's fists pounded on the door, rattling the numbers that looked so secure. "Neil!" When no one answered, he threw them against the door in rapid succession again. "Neil Jones!" His voice didn't even feel like his own. It was like a stranger's anger had built up inside of him and exploded out into the open.

Still no answer. Another pound and the number 6 fell with a *clink* on the cemented front porch. Now the perfect front door matched his former dilapidated one.

"Neil! Open up!"

Richard's voice tore through his throat.

"Open up the—"

The door eased open and Neil's face greeted Richard's. His brows were knitted up in annoyed stitches.

"—door." Richard finished his sentence and lowered his aching arms to his side.

"Richard, I'm sorry I didn't answer the door sooner. I was—" Neil's words came out in one breathless stroke.

"Where's Amy?"

"Excuse me?" Neil's expression softened. His eyes widened in little worried saucers.

"I said, where's Amy?"

Did he not hear?

"Amelia," Neil said, "is … indisposed."

"Indisposed? What exactly does that mean? I haven't seen her in … in a week! That's not *indisposed*, Neil. That's—"

"Richard, you haven't lived here in a week. You moved out, remember?"

"Of course I remember!" Richard's blood grew hot, boiling from the pit up his stomach and rising to his neck. For a moment, he wanted to take a page out of Pigtails' book and spit on the ground, leaving behind a wad of his irritation on Neil's doorstep. "I'm the one who walked out, leaving this dump behind. I had to, I know I had to—" He had to keep Amy safe, right?

There was a sound coming from behind Neil, muffled through one of the doors. A weak, "Neil," slid down the hall and into Richard's ears.

Richard exhaled his concern. His blood cooled and hands unclenched. The butterflies relaxed their agitation. Amy was okay. Her perfect little voice carried over to him, easing his concerns. She was okay.

"Richard, you're drunk. Why don't you go sleep it off somewhere." It wasn't a suggestion. It was a command.

"Neil…" The voice, almost a whisper, called out again. But this time, Amy sounded different. Her voice was gravelier than usual, deeper than her typical songbird timbre. Richard's butterflies started their wings again.

"Or go get some fresh air, huh?"

"Neil." This wasn't a weak whisper anymore. It sounded like someone whining for attention. And it definitely didn't sound like Amy. Now the butterflies were beating their wings full blast.

Behind Neil, a door cracked open. The bedroom door.

Though it couldn't have been the bedroom door, because the woman who stepped out wasn't Amy. In fact, she was the exact opposite. This woman's pin-straight, dark hair hit her waist in silky strands. Her makeup was just as dark, painting her in raccoon eyes and stained ruby red lips. And she was completely naked. Wearing nothing but a coy smile. She wasn't the sunshine Amy was. She was a shadow that slunk in the sunshine's place.

Neil's hand touched Richard's shoulder, pushing him back toward the truck, "Why don't you go for a drive, huh?" His weak commands were starting to strengthen up.

"A drive? A *drive*?" Richard's feet dug into the spot where he stood. The boiling feeling was coming directly from the butterflies flapping, making his blood like the pot of spaghetti sauce on his mother's stove.

Who was this woman, and where the heck was Amy?

"Oh, Neil, you have a friend. That could be *fun*." The dark-haired woman eased out of the bedroom door, touching her bare skin as she looked Richard directly in the eye. "Who's your friend here?"

"Where's Amy?" His two words scratched their way out of his mouth and into the open. His feet stepped inside the apartment, urging for an answer.

The woman picked up a pair of jeans that were crumpled in a mess on the hallway floor. She neatly walked into each leg as she made her way into the living room.

"Hey, *I'm* Alex." She held out her hand after she zipped the jeans together. "Who are *you*?" The complete opposite of Amy's concerned kindness.

"Where. Is. Amy?"

She pulled her hand back and made her way to the couch, the perfect pristine couch, where a white T-shirt lay in a messy bundle. A hooked finger picked it up, and with her back toward Richard, she slipped it over her head. It was like she wanted her bare, pink skin to tell the stories he didn't want to hear.

"Okay, well, *friend to Neil*, since you're not going to give me your name, I suppose I'll have to get *creative*. How are you with games?"

Games? What was this woman talking about?

"Where is Amy?" Though his voice felt weak, he wasn't going to let go of the repeating record track playing from his mouth.

He watched Alex walk into the kitchen and grab a bottle of wine in one hand, two empty glasses in another. Light hit a finger on her right hand and bounced off in blue flickers. It was the ring from the pawn shop. The one Neil had argued about.

The one that was supposed to be for freaking Amy.

It was never for Amy. It was for this woman, Alex. Neil must have sucked up the price tag and come back to pay for it.

But this woman wasn't special enough for a gift meant for Amy.

She didn't radiate warmth like Amy. She didn't smell like vanilla and wildflowers. Her eyes didn't have golden flecks that made Richard's butterflies fly in loops. He didn't want to scoop her up and carry her away from Bridgewell apartments, Samhale County, and take her to somewhere quiet where they could get to know every inch of each other away from Neil.

Alex was a boring average woman who elicited no response from Richard's heart or mind.

"How are you with 20 questions?"

"Where is Amy?"

She sighed, gave Neil a glass, and filled it to the rim with the moscato. He took it with a shrug and sat himself on the couch.

"Good boy," she praised. Then, she filled a second glass and offered it to Richard. "First question, do you like *white wine*?"

His dry mouth answered for him. Before he could send a signal to his hand not to accept the glass in front of him, it was there, and tipped back to his mouth.

"Good, so the answer is yes. Question two. What's your *name*?"

"Where is Amy?" His glass was empty now, and she was refilling it up for him.

"Come off it, Richard." Neil's lazy voice came from the couch. A quick look and his hands were clenched into fists, much like they had been at the pawn shop.

"Ah, so it's Richard. Good, see, we're getting along like old friends now. Question three. What's your favorite game to play?"

Richard's glass was empty again. "I don't understand." Frustration sloshed inside of him, and here was a strange woman who was playing a game of questions, sucking answers out of him without even trying, and he couldn't get the answer to the one question he came here with.

"I'm going to say you're probably a hide-and-seek kind of guy. You're the kind of guy who will hide in the darkness with clenched eyes, hoping no one will find you. But the second someone comes tapping on your shoulder, you're an explosion of defensiveness."

"Where. Is. Amy?"

"Do you have anything to hide, Richard? Anything we need to *seek* out?" She took another sip from the bottle.

"Where's—"

"I told you to shut it, Richard."

"Where is she? Because this isn't her, Neil. This isn't your *wife*." He swung his gaze over to Neil on the couch. The fact Richard couldn't get close to Amy before hurt like hell. But this? Her own husband tossing her aside to give some random woman the attention she deserved? That was unbelievable. "This isn't like you. You're the kind of guy to stand by *her*, support *her*. You're the kind of guy to do right by others. You're not a cheat, Neil. You're not the kind of guy who would...would…"

"Have sex with his wife's *coworker*?" Alex interrupted. Then, she let out a quick laugh. "I guess that's question number four, huh? Kind of?" She shrugged her shoulders and took a swig straight from the wine bottle.

"Her coworker?" Richard's head felt dizzy as he swung it back and forth from Alex to Neil, unable to get out a comprehensive sentence. "You- And she- and the- the- hospital. And - Why?"

More questions bubbled up inside of him, tripping over themselves before they ended out in the open. But he still didn't have the one answer he came for. "Where...where…"

The anxiety and moscato teamed up to overcome him.

His eyes rolled back on the last, "Where," and all he saw was blackness.

CHAPTER TWENTY-TWO

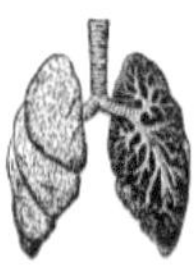

"Guess your game wasn't good enough for him." Neil stood up from the couch and tipped back what was left in his glass. The sweet liquid coated his mouth for a moment longer before he swallowed again and the taste was gone. "At least not good enough to keep him awake."

"Well, that's a real bummer." Alex clicked her tongue as she threw her empty hand on her hip. "Humpf. Well, now what?"

Neil took a few steps toward Richard's body in a heap on the floor, jealous his chest was rising and falling in a recurring pattern. Had he always been able to do that so effortlessly? The lucky jerk. He nudged Richard's side with his foot and watched the body move with the motion.

"Here." Neil handed his empty glass to Alex. "We need to figure out what to do with him. We can't exactly let him stay here, can we?"

She shook her head, silky hair flying by her side. "No; I guess we can't. *Amy* would like that too much, would she?"

Instantly, Neil's jaw clenched. He didn't want to think of *her* right now. *She* had nothing to do with this, with what he could have, what he wanted.

She had already exhausted her worth. He made sure of that when he stuffed her parts in a bag.

No. This wasn't about *her* anymore. This was about the freedom to do what he wanted when he wanted. The freedom he deserved.

Neil went back to nudging Richard's body. "He's put on some weight, hasn't he?"

Alex huffed. "He doesn't look fat to me, Neil."

He darted his eyes toward her, burning a gaze through her words. Here he was, thinking out a plan of action, and she was making quips about the weight of a man she knew nothing about.

"I mean, how would I know? I never met him until today." She rolled her eyes.

Humph. She wasn't wrong. This was the first time she had seen this man, let alone met him. She had no idea how quickly his belly filled with chub. She had never seen him fit with muscles that could carry fallen wood the weight of himself over his shoulders.

And she had never seen the way his eyes watched Amy every time they came face to face with each other — two blue saucers searching for a way to get at her, touch her, hold her. Richard probably shoved his hands down his pants to punish himself every day thinking about Amy.

Richard was like a vulture circling its prey. And the way Amy looked back at him, Neil was sure she would have been happy to lay herself down and be taken by him.

Honestly, that would have been fine with him. If it weren't for the fact that Amy would never actually move to act on it. She took her vows seriously. So Neil took his needs seriously.

Alex cleared her throat. "I wanna do something fun." She pointed to Richard. "He's not any fun just laying down like that. What are we going to do with him like *that*?"

Neil ran a hand through his mopped hair. The only thing he was sure of was he didn't want Richard in his home, crumpled up and rotting on his floor. He'd only wake up and start again with the same broken record as before. Asking questions. Demanding answers. Being nosier than the old woman next door herself.Asking to see *Neil's wife* when he had no business asking for her.

Maybe if Richard was so hard pressed to see Amy, Neil would make it happen. Then, this could be done and over with. But it would be a lot easier with Alex's help.

"I've got an idea." The corners of Neil's mouth turned up when he saw her eyes widen in anticipation. New ideas were always a good way to get Alex excited.

"What is it?" Her hands were clasped together.

"Now, we come up with a new game."

She was an excited kitten, bouncing on her tippy-toes. "Oh, I like the sound of that!" She ran to Neil and wrapped her arms around his neck.

He lifted her up in the air, feeling her feet buck wildly behind her. He pressed his lips against hers and breathed in her giggles. Delicious. Sweet. They'd be even more delectable when he finished this whole thing off for good.

He spun Alex around on the spot and nibbled at her bottom lip. "You ready to play?" His voice growled. He was ready to let her play one more game before they could play together without anyone else bothering them.

She broke into a fit of giggles, bit her lip, and nodded vigorously. "Yes!"

Every day should contain this kind of excitement.

He pinched her sides to draw out a squeal, then placed her feet back on the floor. "Good. You like to drive, right?"

She gave a wide-eyed nod. "Can I drive fast?"

"Baby, you can drive however you want. It's your game."

She slipped a hand under his shirt and stroked his back with her fingernails. "I love it when you talk to me like that."

He bent down, grabbed her jawline in his hands, and forced her to taste his breath. Her desperate moan electrified him all the more. He teased her by stepping backward. His foot landed on Richard's arm, but he adjusted his weight before he could spill the two of them on top of the pile of Teft on the floor. It would be just like Richard Teft to kill the mood.

Her feet followed his suit, stepping toward Neil's body in time. They danced like this, stepping over limbs while tangled in their own until Neil stood still and ran his fingers through her slinky dark hair.

Just as she pulled him in closer, he broke their connection completely.

"Get your shoes on," he said. "We're going for a drive."

Neil left Alex by the front door to search for her shoes while he helped himself to the hall closet. He opened the door and ran his hand along the hangers. Without even looking, he found his sweatshirt right away. His fingertips recognized the familiar worn material.

Slipping it off the hanger, Neil pulled the hoodie over his head. Like a glove.

Gloves.

He wormed a hand into the front pocket. No. There were no gloves to be found. But there was another familiar fabric. One that had imprinted its pattern in his mind. One that forced excited goosebumps down his spine every time he touched it.

"Now what, Neil?" Alex's voice broke him from his concentration.

"What do you mean?" He eased the closet door closed. "Now we get in the car."

"With this?" She pointed down to the Richard-sized lump on the floor.

Neil pushed out as much charm as he could muster in his smile. "Well, it's like you said. We can't just leave him here, can we?"

She grunted as she picked one ankle up and pinned it under her arm. She hoisted the second ankle up and under her other arm with a little more effort. "Well, are you going to help me out?" Her voice squeaked out. "Like you said, this guy has put on a little weight. I can't just drag him out by myself."

"You're right. I was just letting ladies go first."

Neil cracked the front door open and slid both hands under Richard's arms. "One, two," and at "three," he bent at the knees and lifted up. "Easy peasy." He gave her a wink.

Together, the pair walked down the front steps and toward Alex's car. Thankful the old woman wasn't on her front porch for once, Neil let go of his hold of Richard and unlocked the car's back door. With a little extra effort, he dropped Richard's weight into the seat.

They pushed the rest of him in just in time for Gladys's door to open up.

"Neil Jones!" she called out. Her voice was high-pitched, panicked. "Did you get to talk to Richard? Is everything okay?"

Neil smiled and gave her a halfhearted wave. He helped himself into the passenger's side door, ignoring her continued questioning. Alex threw the car into reverse, and he could still hear Gladys yelling after them. Alex shifted into drive and hit the gas pedal hard. Neil was glad to leave the old woman in their wake.

Alex giggled. "Now what? Do we just wait for him to wake up?"

Neil's hand explored the fabric in his hoodie pocket. It was soft and rough. It was smooth and bumpy. His fingers found the embroidery on it, and he traced the stitches as he drew the picture in his mind. It was comfort.

"Now, you drive."

Eventually, Richard would wake up. Eventually, Alex would be able to play. Eventually, they'd find themselves outside the old tree that had called his name, and he'd finally put the last piece of the puzzle away.

"Lavender's blue, diddle diddle."

CHAPTER TWENTY-THREE

Blonde hair wrapped around Richard's fingers. He felt the soft tendrils curl between his knuckles as he combed the hair through his digits. It was like a strand of strong dandelion fluff. It could break off at any moment and get whisked away by the wind. Except, it stayed clinging to its roots.

Entranced, he watched it swish on the floor below him and followed the strands to where they connected. He gazed below where he fixed on a pair of eyes.

Blue. Brown. Hazel. Gray. Green with gold flecks.

They shifted from one color to another. Different sizes. Different shapes. They were a roulette of identities. The dead women on parade. They belonged to Alisha. To Leslie. To Jennifer and Michelle. Morphing from one face to another on repeat. Then they were his mother's.

"Richard, I was going to make you your favorite spaghetti. Richard, remember what I told you about spaghetti sauce? There's no one perfect recipe. No matter how you make it, it'll be good. Spaghetti is always good. But it's only perfect when you can share it with someone else. It was going to be perfect because we were going to share it together, Richard. Lunch was going to be perfect." Her mouth frowned and she blinked her eyes mechanically. "We never had the chance. It probably just boiled over while I was left to die here on the ground. Did you let it boil over, Richard?"

He looked around and saw he was in his mother's bedroom. Barely in the doorframe, he was crouched down next to her, playing with her hair, a pillowcase-less pillow within reach of his hands.

"Oh Momma..." Richard crooned and turned his head behind him. The front door lock, the one he was supposed to replace the broken one with, mocked him from the hallway. His eyes dampened. "Momma, I am so sorry. I should have come earlier. It's my fault."

"Are you ready to take the blame? Are you sure?" Another mechanical blink. When Richard didn't answer, her mouth opened again. "It doesn't matter. It's too late for me anyway."

"And me." Another voice squeaked out, and Richard redrew his focus on the woman's face in his lap.

It was no longer his mother. It was another woman. Her eyes were bright blue and held a fear unlike Richard had ever seen. Her eyes darted from side to side and she muffled a quick, "It's too late for me, too." Then her mouth shaped into a tiny O as she let out a, "No... Noo..NO!" until it became a blood-curdling scream vibrating his ears. Her body didn't move an inch, as her facial features twisted into agitation, panic, and then finally horror.

Richard sat, paralyzed until the lady's scream faded and the face morphed again.

Gray eyes now stared back reflecting his fear in their irises. Her mouth opened to scream some more, but air caught in her throat, and the only sound that came out was a slight gasp as her eyes rolled backward.

His hand reached out and he realized there was sticky red liquid covering it.

Sticky red liquid and blonde strands between his fingers.

Richard blinked again, and a new face was now in front of him.

This woman's green eyes shifted, and the mouth twisted into a familiar grin. One that warmed Richard's heart better than any bottle of bourbon ever could. The face of sunshine itself. Amy Jones.

"Richard. I can't move." Her tiny voice squeaked out.

"Amelia?"

"I can't move, Richard. My arms and legs. They're stuck."

"I don't understand, Amelia. You're right here. Aren't you?" The weight in his lap felt like it was dissipating, becoming light as a feather. He was afraid she was going to disappear into nothingness forever. "Amy ... Where are you?"

"I'm here, Richard. I'm here and I can't move. I can't do anything. I'm so cold." As her mouth moved, a fly crept out of her inner cheek, across a white tooth and over her bottom lip. It sat there, cleaning itself off as if it had just crawled out of an unspeakably dirty trap.

Ignoring the fly, Richard reached down and looped one of her curls through his fingers. It felt like an intrusive move he should have never done. This was never his hair to touch. Guilt washed over him, but the butterflies swung on a trapeze. Finally, he was able to hold her, feel her, have her.

But then something light tapped his head.

Dozens of golden and mustard-colored leaves rained down on him and Amelia Jones, covering them both in blankets of foliage. He looked back down to hold her closer, smell the lavender in her hair, but she was gone. Amy was gone. Richard's mother was gone. All the women were gone.

And in their place was a mound of yellow-blond leaves. He dug at them with his hands, frantically pushing them away to find the face that made his butterflies loop. But for every leaf he scooped to the side, a dozen more piled on his lap. They fell down in droves, cascading over his head and shoulders, and filled up the room around him.

The room. It was no longer his mother's. It was his home. Amy. His Amy. The space filled with leaves, with death.

The last thing he remembered was Neil's apartment and the taste of sickening sweet wine. And then darkness.

His eyes opened, allowing minimal light to pull him awake. The back of two leather bucket seats were in front of him. A car. He was in the backseat of a car. On top of the center console two hands linked their fingers together, polished blue topaz shining from the driver's ring finger.

Alex.

Neil was in the passenger's seat. His black hair danced to wind seeping in from the window. He was admiring Alex at the wheel with a stupid carefree smile that belonged to Amy.

How Richard wished he would have scooped Amy away from Neil long ago, especially now with his making stupid faces at the wrong woman.

"He's awake." Neil's voice came out slick, like the words had been well greased before being released into the open.

"Oh. Hi, Richard." Alex's voice was light, sing-songy. And it wasn't Amy's.

"Hi?" he grunted out. The pounding in his head stopped him from asking the same question that had gotten him nowhere so far.

"Poor thing looks like he's been put through the ringer, doesn't he?" She let out a faded giggle.

"It's good he rested. He'll need to take extra care of himself to make sure there isn't any obvious injury that will pop up later, like a concussion or something." Mechanically, Neil sounded like he had memorized the line after speaking it a thousand times over tirelessly caring for people who needed rest and comfort.

"What … what happened?" Richard rubbed the top of his head to try to clear out a throbbing pain of confusion. The pain shot through his temples and ran down his spine. And Amy still wasn't here.

"Well, we were having some *fun* and I guess you got tired of it." Alex's eyes shot at him from the rearview mirror.

Richard's attention darted from her gaze to the mirror to the two hands holding each other. He watched her hand unlink from Neil's and wondered when those fingertips first touched each other, and if Amy ever knew they did.

"Fun?" He rubbed his head to clear it enough for conversation. "What do you mean, fun?"

Her fluttery giggle seeped out again. "We were playing a game, Richard. But I guess it wasn't *exciting* enough for you. So, me and Neil decided we would play another game. One that might be a little more interesting to you. Maybe, keep you more awake.."

Awake. He did need to keep himself awake. Because if he wasn't awake, if he allowed the darkness to drown him, he was dangerous. Dangerous enough to land himself on Amy's back doorstep. Dangerous enough to create the blonde parade?

"You said you work with Amy." His thumbs worked in circles at his temples. How could someone who knew Amy, who *worked* side by side with her, watching her radiate sunshine on hundreds of patients, betray her by *sleeping with her husband*?

"You got that right. Boring ol' Amy. I always tried getting her out to have fun. You know, go for a few drinks after work, check out the nightlife once in a while. Or just go on a joyride or *something*. But that girl never wanted to do any of the sort. She's always been about doing the good thing, the right thing, the boring thing. I'm pretty sure Neil here has been dying for a break from the monotony of it all, so I gave it to him." She took a breath. "So yeah. We're here to have fun, isn't that right, *Mr. Jones*?"

With eyes closed and a lazy smile, Neil nodded his head, slowly. The relaxed expression looked alien on him.

"What do you mean … fun?" Richard was still rubbing his temples, trying to create some form of focus that wasn't there.

"Oh *you* know, dear. *Fun*." Alex let out a muffled cackle. "I've got a whole new game to play. Are you ready for it?'

No, he wasn't. He didn't want to participate in whatever this was.

"Okay. This game is called one, two, three. I'll count to three, and at *three*, you have to make a decision. There is a definite *right* decision and definite *wrong* one. But you have to make the decision on your own, okay? No cheating. Mr. Jones can't give you any help, either."

"Neil…"

Addressing his used-to-be-neighbor felt like it might be a reach. But it also might have been the easiest way out of this mess, and Richard wanted a one-way ticket out of the car and back to his tree, back to *his* Amy. Where he was comfortable. Where he felt safe and at home. Where he could talk to *his* Amy and come up with another way to find the Amy he never could have… and scoop her away.

"Relax, Richard. Alex is pretty good with games. She's just having a little fun."

Okay, talking to Neil wasn't going to get him out of this either.

"Ready? Here we go." Alex placed both hands on the steering wheel. "One."

Richard watched her with curious eyes, wondering what kind of decision was supposed to come to him in less than three seconds.

"Two…" Alex locked eyes with him in the rearview mirror. She gave him a tiny wink.

"Three!" Both of Alex's hands jerked the steering wheel to the right, then jumped from it without correcting its direction.

The car jolted, bumped over the side road gravel, and was making a straight line for the line of trees.

Richard jumped from his seat and grabbed the steering wheel, correcting it into their lane. "What do you think you're doing? You're crazy!" His heart raced so much that it cleared his head of any leftover haziness from earlier. The butterflies in his stomach felt like they just experienced whiplash.

She put her hands back on the steering wheel. "Not crazy, just enjoying myself. Just playing a game. You can let go now."

"How do I know you're not going to let go again? Let us crash into a tree on the side of the road or headfirst into another car coming the opposite direction?"

"Oh please, none of that is going to happen. I have a severe distaste for hurting people. I just like spending some time with them. Play around a little. See what they do." She gave him a wink. "Besides, in this game, you can't do the same thing twice. It would ruin the surprise."

Unsure, he let go and forced himself to relax in the backseat. His eyes stayed on her hands, though. Just in case.

"Okay, you ready for round two, mister? One…"

Richard kept his eyes on her and whatever sudden movement she might make.

"Two…"

All of the alcohol evaporated from his system. He felt more sober than he had in a long time. The butterflies were at a standstill, still shaking off the effects of the last round.

"Three!"

Richard jolted forward, his arms hitting the back of both bucket seats. His neck and head whipped forward in the same motion. Actual whiplash.

"Tsk, tsk, tsk. You should have put on a seat belt, Richie." She flicked at her own belt across her lap.

"How could I?" Richard barked back, his head swimming with anger. "It's not like I had the time to put one on. And with this stupid game of yours, I need to be ready to jump in and steer the car away from oncoming traffic. Come on, Neil. You've got to do something! We can't be messing around like this. This isn't a game. Someone is going to get hurt."

His hand cupped his neck and rubbed the soreness out of it.

Neil's only response was to shrug, resting his hands behind his head while the car started to move again. It was as if he was enjoying this as much as anyone would enjoy a quiet day in the sun.

Amy. Where was Amy's sunshine now?

"Here we go, round *three*. Let's see if you get this one right!"

Adrenaline pulsed through every vein within Richard. What was this woman's deal?

"Let's see. How should the next round go?" She didn't seem to have a plan thought out for this round. Not yet, anyway.

A slight whirring sound filled Richard's ears and wind hit his face. All four windows were down now, and the furrowed eyebrows he saw in the rearview indicated Alex's mental wheels were turning. He was in the presence of a mad woman.

An idea must have landed somewhere within her, because her brows unknitted and she drew out a cackled exhale. "How's that *head* of yours feeling, Richard? One…"

He sat up straight, his endorphins making his posture rigid. He glanced over at Neil. Why was he so relaxed?

"Neil? What's going on here?"

As if it were possible, Neil sank even more into his seat. "You know, Richard, sometimes you just have to … let loose. It feels so good to not have a predictable schedule handed to you, calling for you to spend nearly every waking minute being a goodie-two-shoes. Fixing up other people's houses. Filling up other people's plates. Running errands and filling in little jobs here and there for everyone else who is more than capable of doing it themselves, yet refuses to do so." He tilted his head to gaze back at Richard. "People just like you, Richard. People who look for the handouts, greedily taking them as they find them. Without remorse, never questioning the sacrifices the people giving them that hand had to make."

Richard rubbed his temples again, keeping Alex within his peripheral vision. "I never asked for a handout, Neil."

Neil leaned his head back on the headrest again. "No, you didn't, did you? But Amy still gave them away freely to you. The goodie bags on your front porch, the little tips to take care of yourself. Had she found out you were kicked out of the apartments like you were, she would have thrown our best sheets on the couch and given up every inch of the living room for you."

"Two…"

The sound of Amy's name made Richard's jaw clench. "Where's Amy?" Finally, the question made its way out again.

"You want to know where Amy is? You don't know yet? I'm surprised you haven't seen her." Neil's expression shifted in an instant. He was no longer the carefree, relaxed man in the passenger's seat. He was just as disturbingly giddy as Alex herself, and as wild as he was that day in the pawn shop.

"Of course I haven't seen her. I've been gone from the apartments, and you've been with…with…" He couldn't bring himself to say the wrong woman's name.

"*Alex*, dear." Alex's head whipped around. "Come on, Neil, I wanted to play. Why are you giving this guy your life story?"

Neil's hand jerked the steering wheel, and Alex let out a giggle while clapping her hands with delight. "Oh, *good*! You *are* wanting to play after all!" The car growled in another jolt forward, indicating her foot pressed even harder on the gas pedal.

Neil's hand continued to swing the wheel right and left, guiding the vehicle along the road from the passenger's seat.

They weren't playing Alex's game anymore. This was a whole new type of game. And there was no telling where this one was going to lead them.

Neil's hand pulled the steering wheel right. They breezed through a stop sign without hesitation. They bumped down the road for a while until Neil yanked it a sharp left, nearly skidding into a van coming from the opposite direction.

Richard watched with wide eyes as they kept on like this, speeding past stop signs, making their way in and out of sharp turns and right down...Whispering Pass.

"Brake, Alex," Neil's voice command.

"But, I'm still having *fun*."

"Brake."

Alex's breath came out as a huff as the car skidded to a screeching halt. Outside the window, Richard saw the tree. *His* tree. His Amy tree.

"Neil, why are we…"

"Everyone. Out." Neil's voice unwavered in its command.

In another huff, Alex killed the ignition. All three people opened their doors and pulled themselves out onto the paved road. The moonlight shone just enough to illuminate the oak tree in front of them and the thick blanket of leaves on the ground. The branches were nearly bare now, open, outstretched, waiting for them to arrive, almost as if they were looking for someone to grab.

"Neil, why are we…" Richard repeated.

"Come. I'll show you." Neil led the way for Richard to follow. Alex trailed behind the men, stomping her feet in a rhythmic temper tantrum.

When they reached the oak tree, Neil extended his arm out. He ran his fingers against the bark and tapped it with his index finger. "Do you know what this is?"

Now it was Richard's turn to huff. Neil's hands violated him, running up and down and over the oak tree… the Amy tree. Neil was touching *his* Amy when Richard never dared to touch Neil's.

"You got kicked out of the apartment and found your way here, didn't you?"

"How … how did you know?"

"Richard, when your wife drags you around to every nook and cranny of Samhale, you get to know Sam Hill everything." Neil let out a gruff chuckle at his own joke. "This community isn't as big as you'd think, you know. If you get pulled into the lives of nearly everyone who lives here, you get to know nearly everyone's business. All the goodie-two-shoes and all those people who made them the way they are."

Richard tried to shake away the millions of questions bubbling in his thoughts. There's only one question he really wanted answered.

"Where's Amy?"

Where *was* Amy?

"Funny thing about Amy. She used to live right over there." Neil pointed to their right. "Just down the road some. And I—" He pointed to their left. "—lived in that direction. But that was ages ago. Before we grew up. Before we knew anything of the world of give and take. We were kids who could just be as we were. Do what we wanted when we wanted and how we wanted."

There was a slight, "Mmm-hmm," that slipped out of Alex's closed lips.

"Right here." Neil kneeled on the ground and pointed to one of the protruding roots. "We used to sit right here as kids. We'd leave our houses and meet in the middle, fantasizing about breaking out of Samhale and exploring the open world." Neil looked up at Richard with dreamy eyes. "You know, there was a time when she believed in castles and fairytales and just having fun for yourself." Neil stood up and walked around to the side of the tree. An incessant buzzing of a million flies became their background noise. "You see this, here?" His index finger trailed along a carving, faded from the tree's attempt to heal itself over time. "N and A. Neil and Amy. I carved this when we believed we could do anything we wanted. I guess when I believed I could do anything I wanted."

Alex's voice broke through the tension. "I guess that A could stand for someone else then, huh?"

"Oh shut up, Alex."

"What? It's not like no one here *doesn't* know by now. *Clearly* things with your little fairy princess aren't working out. Not like I didn't see that coming. She was *always* so *boring* at the hospital. She was always worried about whether or not Mrs. Burns needed a new bedpan or if Mr. Tyler got the right dosage of morphine. I can't tell you how many times she tried to get me to listen to Old Samuel Headel tell another story about his mother's cousin's sister's whatever. It took all day to finally nail down why the heck he was there in the first place. She never wanted to leave her shift early. Never took full *advantage* of the break room. I always tried to get her to come out for a *joy ride* or two, but she was too worried about everyone else in the damn place except her."

"Shut up, Alex."

"Oh, come on. Your wife is *nothing* like you. You crave to be *free* and she's busy strangling you on a short leash."

"I said, shut up, Alex."

"Oh, whatever. I'm bored of this." Alex crossed her arms in protest of the scene in front of her.

Neil ignored her silent objection. "It's pretty funny you chose to relocate right here, at this spot."

"How...how did you know?" Richard asked again as he looked up at his tree house-home, and for the first time felt shame that this was where he was living. This was yet something else Neil had before Richard put his eyes on it.

"It's weird that this tree just keeps calling me back, you know?"

Could Neil hear the whisper, too?

"Neil. I don't want to ask again. Where. Is. Amy?"

Neil's smile widened as he lifted his gaze toward Richard.

"I always saw the way you looked at her, you know. Like you wanted to reach out and take her from me. You win, Richard. I had her, but I'm done with all that now. Now, you can have her. She's yours. I won't even fight you for her. In fact, the two of you can be together. Forever."

"What do you mean?"

Neil pointed to the hollow in the tree, where the buzzing grew louder and the flies darted in and out, smacking their little fly lips with their little fly tongues…

"She's been right here all along."

CHAPTER TWENTY-FOUR

Standing in front of his tree with Neil Jones by his side, Richard felt as naked as Alex when he first saw her.

Neil knew. He knew how he felt about Amy all along. Neil had cut through the veil he had put up for so long to hide his infatuation.

But was that so wrong? Everyone wanted a piece of Amy, because she was so willing to divvy her attention. That didn't make Richard any more special than anyone else. It didn't mean that she would ever reciprocate those feelings. She was devoted to her husband, as any good wife would be. She was a good wife, a good person. So he kept his distance and respected Neil's space when he could. He would have never acted on his impulse. Not without good reason.

Had he known there was good reason all along, he wouldn't have given it a second thought. He would have taken her hand and built a treehouse for two.

"Neil, what do you mean Amy has been here all along?"

There was no direct answer, just a hum that slipped from his pursed lips.

"Neil...?" This had better not be some other game. "What do you mean..."

His humming buzzed louder than the swarm of flies until it broke through and became words, "...diddle diddle..."

Richard put his hand on Neil's shoulder and forced the man's eyes to meet his. "Neil..."

"Geeze, Richard, all that alcohol must have rotted your brain all the way down to nothing. I mean..." He walked around to the back of the tree, ducking under the base of the treehouse as he trailed his finger along the bark.

"...Lavender's blue...diddle diddle..."

When he reached the opening to the big hollow, an unnaturally wide grin twisted his features. "I mean she's been *here* the whole time."

His singing grew even louder, "I heard one say, diddle diddle...."

With a heavy stomach, Richard thought back to when he saw the hollow for the first time — when he imagined climbing in himself just to see if a person could fit.

"Come *on*, Neil. I'm so bored out here. I wanna go do something *fun*." Alex's voice grew louder as she inched her way closer to the two men examining the hollow. "And it stinks out here, too." She covered her nose. "Neil?"

Neil continued to ignore her. "You might need this, though, if you want to see." He pulled his phone from the pocket of his sweatshirt and clicked on its light. The bright yellow beam pierced through the sky and with an audible smirk, Neil swung it around to shine into the hollow.

"I heard one say, diddle diddle... since I came hither..."

Richard couldn't comprehend what his eyes were seeing.

Hungry flies feasted on a fleshy clump. Flies that weren't so lucky to get a taste buzzed in and out of the hollow, urging for their turn.

Richard's stomach dropped. His hands broke into a sweat. The butterflies inside him crumpled their wings. Beyond the moving black mass of insects was a tangled mess of blonde hair and dirt. Coagulated blood coated the tendrils, sticking it to the shape of a face underneath. Two cherub cheeks, a dimple of a nose, plump little lips that dipped into the shape of a heart. And green eyes that had lost their golden flecks.

"That you and I, diddle diddle!"

Amy Jones had been here all along. Dismembered and shoved into the hollow of his Amy tree.

"Shall lieeeee..."

He jerked himself away and fell to his knees. His chest tightened as he closed his eyes, trying to steady his breaths. But closing his eyes didn't erase the image he just saw. It multiplied. Flashes of curly blonde hair. The hair of Alisha and Leslie. The hair of Jennifer and Michelle. The parade of women who plagued his dreams and lingered in the moments right after his blackouts. And now Amy had joined the parade.

"Together!"

Vomit lurched from the pit of his stomach and spread over the leaves below him.

Closing his eyes, he could still see the matted hair. Amy's hair.

Amy Jones *had* been with him. She had been here, cold, begging for warmth.

And it wasn't by his hands.

He breathed out a sigh of relief when the realization hit him. Amy didn't die by his hands. Neil's gross display of proud performance proved it.

"Come on, Richard. Isn't this what you wanted? Now, you can have her. I'm done. I had her. And then I *had* her. Just the way I wanted, too. Her last breath was the most delicious one of all. And the most rewarding."

"How long?" On hands and knees, Richard barked up at Neil, who was now back to dancing to his creepy song.

"Lavender blue...."

"How. Long. Neil?" The sickness grew in his stomach, covering the butterflies in acid and bile. Amy had been cold. Neil took away her warmth. He took away her breath. *His* Amy was *Neil's* Amy, after all, and he still couldn't save her.

Neil said nothing. His vocal cords quieted and his lips pursed together again. The humming persisted, but lower, to almost barely a sound at all.

"Neil, I—" Alex's voice dropped to a meek timbre. "Did you really—" She didn't sound like the carefree, careless woman behind the wheel of the car anymore. "—kill her?"

Neil tossed his phone in a wide arc to her. As she instinctively caught it, he let out a heavy breath. "What do you think? Is this wild enough for one of your games?"

She took a step back and shook her head. "No, Neil. I never wanted to *kill* anyone. Just...just *scare* them, play around a little bit. I thought we were having fun. I thought—"

"We *were* having fun, Alex. We've been having fun. And now … now I can finally breathe. I can be free to do anything whenever I want however I want. Now that I don't have anyone smothering the life out of me, I am free. And now we can do all the playing we want."

"Geeze, Neil. I knew she was bad for you, but I never expected you to *kill* her. That's just … that's too far, Neil."

"It was more than her." Richard's voice felt foreign in his throat as it dragged its way out into the open. "It was all of them."

There was a *wispt* as the phone fell from Alex's hands and into the dead leaves by her feet. "What do you mean, *all* of them?"

"All of them. Alisha, Jennifer, Michelle … all the women in the news with the pretty blonde hair. The women who everyone in Samhale loves and adores. The women with smiling faces who help the community with volunteer hours and selfless love. They were all done in by his hands." He swallowed back the sickness threatening to shake from the butterflies' wings and spill out into the open. "Weren't they, Neil?"

Neil scoffed. Clearly it wasn't his plan to recount every step he took, every window he broke into, or every breath he stole for himself.

Richard pushed the sickness down further, ordering it to remain at the butterflies' feet. "I'll take that as a yes. And for what? So you could knock your rocks off a little? So you could get out of a couple of charity events?"

"So I could *breathe*, you idiot. She was suffocating me. And every face that looked like hers and every voice that sounded like hers. They all did the same. They all suffocated me. They kept doing it and doing it until I finally beat them to the punch line." He took in a deep breath as proof. "But it never failed. I'd come back home and my short-lived freedom ended again. But now…" He exaggerated a few more deepened breaths. "See? Now, I can breathe just fine. I cured myself." That upturned smile was so smug.

"The Samhale Strangler." Alex's face dropped as she took tentative steps backward. "The Samhale Strangler," she repeated, and as Neil made an attempt to walk after her, she quickened her pace. "You're the Samhale Strangler."

It was like watching a game of tag, only the tagger was an insane murderer after the sunshine itself and the person he was playing with no longer wanted to be in the game.

Neil stretched his arms out to his side as he took another step toward her. "Oh come on now. There's nothing standing in our way, Alex. Nothing. No Saturdays at the children's hospital wing. No Wednesday night food drives. No more week-long projects trying to make someone else's crappy house into a more presentable dump." He inhaled deeply enough Richard could hear the air enter his lungs. "My time is open and free. I am free! We can play all the games you want.

"Even this..." Neil tossed his thumb to the tree. "Even this is a little game in itself, isn't it? Like, Cat and Mouse. Only I'm playing both sides. I've already caught all my mice and now it's time to hide away from the blue badged cats."

Alex was a little mouse herself, scurrying her feet as fast as she could while keeping her eyes on the predator in front of her.

"And, honestly, that's going to be the easiest part of the whole thing. People have been talking in this neighborhood. People think the 'contractor' in the white pickup is a creepy man to look out for."

The little mouse tripped over something in the foliage, but she recovered quickly. Would she get away?

"Just one call and the police are going to swarm around this tree, ready to arrest the creepy drunk who everyone is already suspicious of."

Neil, the cat, crept toward her. If he had a tail, it would twitch in tiny zigzags behind him.

"I'm a winner, Alex. I've won every game we've played together. And I'll win at this one, too. In fact, I already have."

Alex hit her back on the hood of her car. Now, she was the scared mouse with a way out, as long as she found her little mouse hole and scrambled into it. Her hand stuck out behind her, fumbling blindly for the handle entry to her little mouse hole. "You're crazy. Stay back. Stay back!"

Success. She gained access and slid into the driver's seat, closing up the door to the mouse hole of a car. Richard could still hear her yelling from the inside of her car, a muffled squeak that was scurrying away.

"Crazy bitch," Neil muttered.

Richard spat at the ground, surprising himself with a new habit of disgust. "Even crazy people have to draw a line somewhere. Looks like you found where her line is. And you crossed it how many times?" Alone with Neil, his body shook. Every doubt he had on himself was actually meant for Neil, the nice guy who showed up to help alongside his wife. The butterflies asked him for a drink. Just a taste. Just something to make the sickness stay at bay.

"Enough times for it to do the trick." Neil's voice sounded lazy. "You know, I didn't want to do it. Not at first, but once I realized how much relief I felt, I didn't feel so bad, you know? It was like popping the cork of a bottle of champagne to release the pressure that had built up over years of suffocation."

Those bottles called to Richard now from the corner of his little treehouse. Maybe one tiny bottle would stop himself from shaking. Maybe it would clear his mind enough to figure out how to handle whatever would come next with Neil Jones, the Samhale Strangler, and how to avenge the Sunshine he missed so much. Just a sweet taste of sticky bourbon would do the trick. Methodically, he pulled himself up in the treehouse.

"Hey Richard, so how's it been living out here, huh? Any better than the Bridgewell complex?"

Richard ignored Neil's calls. He didn't want to face this man. He wanted the moment to be fixed. And even though he knew nothing in his box was going to fix it, he answered to the bottles anyway. It promised to relieve some of the pressure that was building within him. Maybe it would help him make sense of what he was facing. A fix would come after that.

"Richard? You hear me up there? I want to see where you'll be sharing your space with my wife!" Neil's chuckle rang from the ground below him.

His hand reached over to his box and fished out a bottle. As he pulled it closer, a gust of wind blew through the doorway opening, and he could hear the fallen leaves on the ground adjust their positions.

He thought he could hear a whisper, too, behind Neil's fits of giggles.

Amy's whisper.

As he unscrewed the cap, the whisper grew louder. "*You need to breathe,*" it echoed in his ears.

He took a deep inhale and blew it out, trying to understand its meaning.

"Richard Teft!" Neil's voice grew from its faded tone in the background — from lower than a whisper and crawling into focus.

"*You need to breathe, too,*" it said again.

Two hands slapped the floor of the treehouse. Neil had followed him inside. His cockiness had gotten the best of him and here he was, sitting in front of Richard, a proud smile playing on his face for everything he accomplished. "Not too bad for a humble abode. Moving on up, are we?" Neil chuckled as he drew himself next to Richard on the floor. "Well, except for the creepy bags on the wall. What's up with that?"

"*Breathe, Richard.*" The whisper was begging him to do something about it. Shut Neil up for good and create relief for himself and for *her.*

Richard screwed the cap back on the bottle and chucked the whole thing at the floor. It loosely cracked, and liquid seeped out. He hadn't even tasted it.

"Whoa there, slugger. Be careful or you're going to hurt someone with that temper of yours."

Richard's breaths came hard and heavy. How did he end up here? A grown man, living in a treehouse, built within an oak that held the body of one of Samhale's only Sunshine? Now, sharing the space with the Samhale Strangler himself. The butterflies wrapped themselves around his heart and tightened their wings. As he locked eyes on Neil's, he realized his Amy was right. He'd have to do something to let himself breathe again.

His hand found the plastic smile on one of the closest bags and ripped it off the wall. "This? You think this is creepy?" He ripped another off the wall. "This is protection." And another. "Protection from the cold." Two more flew off in swift rips. "Protection from the outside world." Richard grabbed one more and slowly untacked it, pulling it closer to him as he dropped to his knees next to the Samhale Strangler. "Protection from you."

Richard reached his hand inside the bag and began pulling out the stuffing. Leaves danced like butterflies in the air around them. One by one, they fluttered to the ground. Each time they hit, he heard the familiar whisper again. *"Breathe."*

"Who was the first, Neil?" His heart wanted to break free of the butterflies' grasp and tear through his chest. "Who started this whole twisted thing off? Amy was the last, I'll make sure of that. But who was the first?"

Neil dropped backward on his elbows, relaxing his body in a lounging position. Clearly he had no concerns over Richard, Alex, Amy, or anything else anymore. He was truly the most relaxed Richard had ever seen him, like he was on permanent vacation from all the cares that were forced on him. "I think you know the answer to that, Richard."

"Say it."

"You really want me to? It feels like so long ago. I'm not sure it even matters."

"Say. It."

Neil sighed and rolled his eyes. "It was your mother, Richard." He adjusted himself again, now lying on his side. How could he be so nonchalant about this? So relaxed and dreamy? "Remember at the barbeque? You talked all about the problems with her door. It wouldn't lock, would it? Amy reminded me all about it when we were volunteering at a house for Habitat for Humanity. She dragged me along to one of these decrepit, falling-apart homes. Some sad old man living there on disability. His door didn't lock either.

"All I could think about was getting out of that stupid house and relaxing at home. I wanted to be free of the old man's place that smelled like mold and hand cream — that kind of smell would make your stomach turn. But this had been on her stupid calendar for months. It was there. In stone. Just like all the other meetings and volunteer groups and little tasks she promised me I would attend.

"That night, I couldn't sleep. I kept thinking about that stupid doorknob. I should have left right then. Amy told me where she lived, you know. She was determined to drag me around to help if you couldn't get to it right away. She knew you wouldn't. There's just something about you that promised you wouldn't. When Amy was fast asleep in bed, I could have easily left, but I didn't. Something kept me right there, next to her, stewing in all this." He gestured irritably to his head.

"By morning, I was so tired I couldn't even think. And I felt like I couldn't even breathe. I decided to go for a drive, choking on every bit of air. I don't know how I got there. I'm not even sure I knew I was at the right place. I guess the address just burrowed down and stuck in my memory, but I was too tired and too suffocated to think straight.

"I walked in. Just helped myself through the door. You hadn't been there at all. It had been weeks since you told Amy, and you still hadn't gone. I guess I can thank your laziness for that. She had the stove on. The whole place smelled like a damn Italian deli. Who makes spaghetti in the middle of the day like that?" A smile slid across his face. "I think she thought I was you. She called your name. I thought about answering her, but before I did, she ran straight to her bedroom."

The picture of Emily Teft on the floor ripped through Richard's heart, scattering his butterflies in all directions. Had he been there like he had promised, this wouldn't have happened. Even if he had gotten there earlier in the day, just a few hours earlier, he could have done his job. He could have protected her. He could have been sitting at the table with her, enjoying a too-early bowl of spaghetti with his mother.

"Her hair is what got me. She almost looked like Amy from behind. That's not what I had planned. In fact, I didn't plan anything. It's like her address was on my calendar just like anything else, and I got there on autopilot. She was another task to tick off. Another thing that needed doing. But when I saw her hair, I choked. It felt like the air around me was so thick I couldn't swallow it down. *She* had suffocated me for so many years, so I did the only thing I could think of."

Neil reached into his hoodie pocket and let a piece of the fabric inside slip out. Blue embroidered lavender springs. They matched Emily Teft's bedspread perfectly. The pillowcase-less pillow wasn't missing its case by mistake. It had been in Neil's possession this whole time.

Neil leaned forward. "Did you know it takes about five minutes for a person to stop breathing while being suffocated by a pillow? Something magical happened after those five minutes. Five and a half minutes, actually. She was a fighter, just had to hang on for an extra thirty seconds. The moment she stopped, I could breathe again. I wasn't choking anymore. Everything was clear as day, and I wasn't suffocating."

As Neil closed his eyes and took in another deep breath, all of Richard's thoughts stopped completely. His body acted for him.

He lunged across the floor, knocking his full weight into Neil's. Caught off guard, Neil shielded himself with one arm. Richard grabbed it and twisted it to the floor, pinning it down under his knee.

Neil's other arm struggled underneath him. Richard shifted his weight just enough to pin it under his other knee. Now it was like he was kneeling on two bony pillows. It caught him off guard as to how easy this was – to restrain the Samhale Strangler. The fact that he could in a few simple sweeps made him even angrier. Had he stopped focusing on his own inner demons, he could have stopped the Samhale Strangler from doing his damage a long time ago.

Before *she* joined the parade.

Before the parade ever started.

Richard's chest felt like it was caving in on itself. An invisible vise clamped around his lungs, making it impossible for him to steady his breath. The butterflies crumpled to the bottom of his stomach, starved for air, too. Looking at Neil's wide-eyed expression, there was no question on what Richard had to do. He had to take Neil's last breath for himself, and for all the women in the parade. For Amy.

The empty bag in his hand crumpled in delight. In one swift motion, he popped it open and slipped it over Neil's head, tying the looped ends together in a neat bow under Neil's chin, turning him into a present for Richard. The yellow smile readily accepted its duty.

Richard smiled, too. This was also a present for Amy. She had no use for jewelry or fruit baskets filled with oranges, but she could use some justice for herself and for the other women who had their last breaths stolen.

He watched Neil thrash his head back and forth, trying to move out of the plastic captivity. It seemed so odd of a movement compared to the calm and collected manner Neil was just in, telling his gruesome story in delight.

Richard slipped his phone out of his back pocket and watched the time. 11:47 PM.

"You know, Neil, you were supposed to be a protector — as Amy's husband and as a promising Samhale community member. You were supposed to keep harm away from others. That's what you were meant for. That's what Amy wanted you to be."

11:48.

"You weren't supposed to be the selfish husband who literally took the last breath of others for himself. Maybe I couldn't save my mother. Maybe I couldn't save Amy or any of those other women." But then there was Pigtails and her friends. Her mother with blonde hair. Other women and girls who could have ended up on Neil's list as easily as Leslie or Michelle.

11:49.

"But I can help protect the rest of this community from you. The breaths you took were never meant for you, and I'm taking them back. For them."

11:50.

Richard didn't know if Neil could hear him through the thin plastic or not, but it didn't matter. As Neil's body slowed down its jerking movements and the mixed smell of feces and urine filled the little treehouse, Richard realized he wasn't speaking out loud for Neil's sake. He was speaking it for Amy's.

11:51. Four minutes. It felt good to know that his mother had more fight in her than Neil did.

His chest rose as he filled his lungs for his mother, for Amy, and for all the other women whose breaths were taken from them. As he stood up, he exhaled, knowing all of Samhale's caregivers could continue to protect their community, each other. And women like Pigtails' mother wouldn't have to dye their hair. Pigtails herself could grow up without worrying about her appearance either.

The corner of the room still held his box of liquid comfort, and for the first time in over three months, he didn't have to wonder if he needed it or not. He knew he didn't. His mouth wasn't even dry. It was satisfied and craved nothing.

He picked the box up, ready to dump it, destroy it for all of its worth. It had done its damage, and he was ready to move forward and repair himself the best he could. As he shuffled the box around and stepped over Neil's body, he was ready to move on from this place so Samhale could move on, too.

The moonlight flickered through the treehouse opening, illuminating the mess around him. New flies waltzed between the walls and through the light, thankful for another meal to feast on. He watched the light dance along the discarded bags and tossed leaves. But it moved quicker than moonlight would. It scattered around the floorboards in rapid movements like hyperventilating spotlights.

That's funny, he thought. From here, the flickering light looked colorful, not the typical pale moon reflections. Relentless streaks of red and blue lit up his home and Neil's body on the floor like a Fourth of July basement parade.

"Samhale Police. Come out with your hands up."

CHAPTER TWENTY-FIVE

The cold metal stung around Richard's wrists. He had never felt handcuffs before and was surprised as to how tight they made his shoulders, pulled back with his hands out of sight.

He didn't protest his arrest. He knew exactly how guilty he looked, and how guilty he was. Neil's body was lying still on the treehouse floor, the bag still tied neatly around his head now as a gift to Samhale County. It wouldn't take a genius to figure out what happened inside just a few short minutes ago … twenty, according to the clock on the dashboard. Even the Samhale police, notorious for overlooking the obvious, could see the situation clearly. Regardless, Richard had fallen into Neil's trap and dug himself even deeper into it.

Forceful hands guided him into the back of the police cruiser, and Richard leaned his head back to allow the flashing lights wash over him. It didn't matter what happened to him now, as long as Neil Jones was no longer taking other people's breaths. He'd take responsibility for his actions and let them assume Neil's actions were his own. Richard didn't need justice for himself when he already claimed justice for the women.

He closed his eyes, expecting an officer to jump behind the wheel any minute and drive him away where he'd wait behind cement walls and a set of bars for a trial sentence. But it didn't happen. He could feel how still the empty air was becoming around him.

He opened his eyes to look out the window at the scene in front of him. It wasn't that long ago that he was sitting in this same spot, in his truck, marveling at the potential of that huge oak tree. Now, it just looked sad, like the life from it had been taken away, too. He didn't blame tree-Amy. She had held more devastation than should be allowed.

And now the neighborhood of Whispering Pass would be safer for girls like Pigtails to skate around whenever they wanted without the worry of coloring their hair with smelly dye.

Pigtails. He must have been thinking about the curious kid in detail, because he swore to the left, there was a girl tugging on a police officer's arm who looked just like her. The officer nodded his head at her, moving at the pace of attentive acceptance. And when the girl turned her head to the car, Richard realized it was her after all. Pigtails was out in the middle of the night, showing up at the right place, right time, twenty-one minutes past midnight.

Pigtails looked over at Richard in the car and gave him a quick thumbs up. She had kept the promise she made the first time he met her. "My eyes are open, mister. I'm keepin' them on you."

"Well, that's the last of it." Good Ol' Dave pointed to the last of the oak roots being carted to the tree chipper.

"Thanks, Dave. I appreciate it."

"I'm pretty sure Samhale appreciates it after what happened." Dave's concern bled through his expression.

Richard nodded. That was exactly why he called Dave out to bring a couple of the guys with their equipment to rid Whispering Pass of the nightmare. He tore down the treehouse himself after authorities helped Amy out of the uncomfortable hole, laying her to rest in a plot behind the church on Bridgewell Avenue.

The house nearby bore a Sold sign in the front yard. He heard there was a family moving in with kids around Pigtails' age. They didn't need nightmare stories told to them through the rustling leaves of the oak in their backyard.

"Say, you think you'll come back to work? I'm sure even Puntz can agree you're in a much better place after … everything." Dave crossed his arms, waiting for a response.

Richard chuffed. "I don't think I'd come back even if Putz begged on his knees for it. He'd forever hold all this—" Richard gestured in the air around him "—over my head. No thanks. I think it's time for me to move on from this place anyway."

Dave hung his head. "They only took you for a couple of days. And you walked out an innocent and sober man. Thanks to the local papers, we all know how much of a hero you are by now. No one can hold it against you."

"I'm no hero, Dave."

Riding away in the back of a police car, Richard had thought there would be no question about his guilt. But apparently Pigtails had told the police everything she knew. That kid knew more than any kid should. More than she ever let anyone know. And she had held onto that information until she needed to burst it out into the open.

The butterflies drooped their wings knowing she watched Neil carry Amy's pieces from the woods, dragging her in a duffel bag to where he was going to frame Richard.

Apparently, she had also told the police about watching a 'creeper' sneak into a woman's house through a window. She was so detailed in describing him at the houses he broke into, there was no question as to who it was. She told them about his mop-like hair and the hoodie he was always wearing. She described his voice as man-like and scary from singing a children's nursery rhyme in the woods. The amazing thing was, she had been more worried about getting in trouble with her mom than anything else. Kept saying that she didn't want to get caught sneaking in and out of her window.

She even showed them where Alex dropped Neil's phone and left it there to drive away as quickly as she could. There was more than enough incriminating evidence within the device. Text messages between Neil and Alex proved his anger and motivation against Amy. Neil had confessed his love to his mistress and promised Amy wouldn't be a problem any longer. Their conversations with each other was a long running confession.

Two policemen climbed the treehouse to find Neil's lifeless body under a scattering of leaves, a yellow smiley face painted over his own. Patting down his clothes, they found Emily Teft's pillowcase, lined in a layer of plastic and covered in Neil's fingerprints and DNA. All of this overruled whatever Richard did up to Neil Jones's last breath.

"Well, if you ever change your mind, you know where my number is. I'm happy to back up your character if Puntz gives you a side eye or anything."

"Thanks, Dave."

Dave joined the rest of his crew at their work truck, and Richard watched them pull away. He walked back to his own truck, where a young tree sapling waited. Three tiny oranges were already forming on its branches. He lowered the gate to pull it out when he heard the familiar sounds of a skateboard and the chatter of a couple of voices.

"Emily Ellis, don't you go too far ahead of us, you hear?" one of the voices called.

Pigtails stepped off her skateboard and kicked it up under her arm. "Got it, Mom."

"So, Emily huh?" Somehow, it made sense to Richard.

"Yup. That's me. But you can call me Mills. I kinda like it better that way."

Richard may not have been able to save Emily Teft from Neil's hands, but providing a safe community for this Emily gave him permission to finally let go of the last bit of guilt his butterflies kept hostage.

"Well, you know what, Mills, I have somethin' for ya." Richard crossed his arms and gave her his best smirk that mimicked hers.

She gave one back. "Oh yeah?"

"Yeah." He dug his hand into his pocket and fished around until he found the familiar ribbed metal. "Here."

She held out her hand to accept it. "A...dime?" She looked confused. He nodded. "A dime."

"Uh, thanks for the ten cents, I guess." Mills shoved the dime into her own pocket as she wrinkled her brows.

"Well, it's not exactly ten cents," Richard corrected her. And when she scrunched her face up in even more confusion, he continued. "If you look at...Roosevelt, you'll see there's something missing."

"Huh. So it's messed up?"

"Not messed up."

She tapped her chin in contemplation, and after a moment, her face melted into a look of understanding. "I get it. It's a special dime, different from any others huh? I bet you can get a pretty penny for that if you find the right person to buy it."

This girl was already ahead of where he was when he first touched the dime.

"Yup, you know that saying, 'it ain't worth a dime'? Well, this dime is proof that even the things that don't look like they're worth much can be worth a lot more."

"I get it, mister. You're telling me to keep my eyes open so I can see which things are special and which aren't. Got it." She saluted him.

"Emily, who are you talking to up there?" the voice called again. This time, Richard could tell it was the same two women who were power walking when he first met them.

"No one scary. Promise, Mom!" She rolled her eyes over to Richard. "They seem to think that the creep going around hurting people is going to come back. I keep telling her that the creep is gone. He ain't coming back. But she dyed her hair anyway, and makes me keep my helmet on to cover mine just in case." She tapped the side of her red and black helmet. "She won't let me dye mine, though. Not that I want to. That stuff smells funny and gives me a headache." She gave a halfhearted shrug. "Whatcha doing there?"

"Oh, just a little orange tree. I thought it might be nice for your new neighbors to have one close by. You know, something good for ya."

"You do know that's not their yard, right? That little bit of land doesn't belong to any of the houses. It's like neighborhood land. Mom calls it 'common ground'."

So he had been right. This was an easement. "Then I guess it'll feed the whole neighborhood."

"Good. I like that."

"I like that, too."

"There you are, Emily. You know your mother and I aren't as fast as you are. It's like running a marathon trying to keep up with you." The brunette woman looked up at Richard. "Oh hi. You're the contractor from before, aren't you? You must have done a pretty good job on the rest of the house. I talked to the new neighbors who are moving in next week. They seem pretty happy with what they saw."

"Yeah, they're excited to move in," the other woman spoke up. Richard noticed her hair was tied back the same way it was before, but it was now a deep chestnut color, and she wasn't constantly fondling it.

"Well, I'm glad to hear that." He nodded at her.

"All right, Mills. We've caught our breaths. Why don't you go on ahead and a little down the street, and me and Mrs. Beasley will catch up with you. Just keep your eyes open on the road ahead of you."

"My eyes are always open, Ma. Wider than you'd think." And with that, she dropped her skateboard to the ground and sped away.

"That girl. She's tough as nails, I tell you."

Richard nodded his head in agreement. "She seems like a good kid. You have a good day, ladies."

"You, too, mister. And thanks for taking that old creepy tree down. Not even a treehouse was going to make that thing good to look at. It was just creepy all the way around."

As the two women chased after Emily in their fluorescent '80s leg warmers, Richard scooped up the little sapling in his arms and carried it over to the freshly turned soil. With absolute care, he pushed aside a few inches of dirt and placed the sapling inside. A few more handfuls covered up its delicate roots, providing a space for it to grow a strong foundation. He stepped back to admire the tiny thing.

"Well, Amy. I finally did it. After all the hell you and this town went through, I'm finally doing something that will help out others." He sucked in a deep breath. "I'm sorry I didn't do something sooner. I'm sorry I wasn't in a state where I could. But I promise, I will do better. I will be better. No more drinks. No more feeling sorry for myself. I'm going to start thinking more about others … and breathe. Because I know that's what you'd do, Amy."

He patted the top of the soil, watched a butterfly fly past the new plant, then made his way back to his truck, where his small box of possessions waited for him in the passenger's seat. It was a lot lighter now. No false confidence in liquid form in sight.

Drumming the steering wheel, he thought about his promise to Amy, to himself, to think of others first. His plan was to hit the road and see where it took him. Start over somewhere new. Be impulsive, but in a good way, in a positive way. Be a part of a community the same way all those lost women had always been. Honor them with his breaths, because they couldn't with theirs.

But maybe he should start where it felt familiar.

It didn't take long before he found himself in front of the Bridgewell Apartments welcome sign. Parking in front of number 77, he saw Gladys's empty rocking chair. With his old apartment vacant and the Joneses gone, Gladys didn't have a resource for gossip. But Richard knew she'd still want a story to tell.

He helped himself out of the truck and up her front porch. The smell of cigarette smoke somehow seeped into the cement cracks on her steps. Every time he stepped down his foot, a puff of smoky air reached his nose.

Looking to his right, he took in the faded 8 on his old front door. He half expected a flood of memories to rush through him, but they never did. This was never home. Those walls never held pieces of his life he ever needed to recall. Or wanted.

To his left, the now empty apartment that was supposed to hold all the cheerfulness Samhale could handle within four walls. Yet, there's no telling how empty it actually was before the Joneses had faded from existence.

Knock Knock Knock.

And here Gladys was, positioned between the two empty apartments. The only bit of life left on this row of units.

Woof. Woof.

Well, except the corner tenants with their dogs.

"I'll be damned, it's Richard Teft!" In Gladys Nightingale fashion, she opened the door in a head full of curlers and a cigarette dangling from the corner of her mouth. The TV in the background was loudly playing one of her soap operas. A woman named Jane was yelling a monolog about an evil twin.

"Already seen this one." She shut the door. "What's up, Richard? You miss this place or somethin'? Why are you gracing me with your presence?"

Richard scratched the back of his neck. "I just wanted to see how you were doing."

"Bullshit," Gladys coughed out. "Tell me, is it true what they're saying on the news? You put a stop to the crap that *thing* did?" She jabbed her thumb to where the Joneses used to live.

Richard motioned for her to sit on her rocker. He leaned himself against the handrail and took in a deep breath.

He told her everything he knew. From the moment he walked in on his mother's body to the moment Neil Jones confessed to him on the treehouse floor.

He told her all about little Emily Ellis and how she reminded him of a young and spunky Gladys. He told her how Mills snooped around at night on her skateboard to collect information and give it to the police.

He told her about chopping down the tree and planting something that would take care of the neighborhood kids in its place. Oranges, the sunshine of fruit.

When he was done telling her the last detail, she stubbed out her cigarette on the arm of her chair. "I'll be damned. It is true then." She drew in a breath and leaned her head back. "I never did like him, you know?"

"Me neither."

She scoffed. "Well, no. You wouldn't. You had eyes for his Mrs."

Richard wrinkled his eyebrows. "I like to think it's more than that, now. Turns out he was a pretty big creep."

She nodded her head. "Yeah, he was. But it's even more than that." She straightened her back up. "After all, between the two of you quiet men, you're the one who finally told me a story worth telling. I've been waiting my whole damned life for something good like that, and no one has given me the time of day long enough to actually give me something good. Tells you a lot about someone's character, doesn't it?"

"I guess so. But he was still awful."

"No crap," she agreed. Then, after a brief pause, "So, what now, Mr. Hero? What's next on your plan?"

Richard scrunched up his face. "Well, I doubt Laurel will let me back here even if I wanted."

"I'm sure she'd make an exception for Samhale's finest."

He shook his head. "Nah. I need to go somewhere else. Start over. Find a place that feels more like home, ya know?"

She nodded. "Where's that?"

He shrugged his shoulders. "I guess I'll just find a name on a map. Sounds like heaven to me."

Gladys gave him a thumbs up. There wasn't anything left for either of them to say.

In the driver's seat, he pulled out his phone and drew up the map app from his home screen. He zoomed out as far as it would let him while still keeping roads visible. Without a plan, anywhere would be fine. Anywhere would be worth the trip.

He closed his eyes and let his finger land randomly on the screen. He opened them.

Soura Heights. Guess that was where life was taking him next.

BOOK CLUB DISCUSSION QUESTIONS

1- What detail gave away the killer?

2- What do you think the first interaction between Neil and Alex was like?

3- Where do you think Richard would have ended up if he didn't build himself a treehouse?

4- What do you think is waiting for Richard in Soura Heights now that he's leaving Samhale County?

5- Is there a scene that stands out to you stronger than any of the others?

6- What do you think Gladys was like as a younger person?

7- What's one thing that feels "special" to you from this story?

8- Is there a piece of advice from Richard's mother that resonates with you most?

9- What kind of impact did this story leave on you?

10- Do you think you would ever come back to reread it?

Did you enjoy this book?

I really hope you enjoyed reading *BreathTaken* as much as I enjoyed writing the story of Richard. If you did, I would really appreciate you **leaving a review on either Amazon or Goodreads (or both!)** to help other readers determine if the book is meant for them.

Thank You!

What to read next:
The Fallen in Soura Heights

Want to connect?
I'd love that too!

You can connect with Amanda on social media:
Instagram: @Amanda.B.Jaeger
Website: AmandaBJaeger.com

ACKNOWLEDGEMENTS

If you've heard me talk about my writing process before, you know that my characters talk to me. They come to me with strong voices and a story. Which means, I don't create these stories, my characters do.

However, it takes more eyes on the writing and more hearts in the process to make it the full length finished novel you just enjoyed.

First and foremost, I want to thank my husband for being my rock. Your support through this publishing process has given me the stability I needed to bring my dream into reality. And even though this isn't the kind of thing you enjoy reading, you're still there to cheer me on every single step of the way.

My kids. Girls, even though you haven't had a peek at this one (that I know of), I appreciate every ounce of the both of you for understanding how much writing means to me. Selfishly (or maybe not so selfishly) I love seeing myself rub off on you. I've seen the stories you've started. I've heard the goals you've made for yourself. I'm excited to see your own writing journeys start now. Who knows where you'll end up with them in the future.

To my parents and extended family: thank you for your support. Even without diving into this story before its published date, you've rooted for its success. I'll forever be thankful for you being my lifeline cheerleaders.

Thank you to YOU… my readers. Thank you for reading and taking a chance on me and my work. Your time is valuable and the fact you chose to spend some of it on little 'ol me fills me up with more gratitude than you'll ever know.

My alphas and betas: Leigh, Skyler, Harriet, Emily, Mariette, The Other Emily, Donna, and Tracy. Thank you for giving me your time and efforts to help me strengthen the characters and plot where they needed a little extra oomph. I appreciate all the constructive criticism you gave and I'm glad you didn't hold back.

Thank you to Leslie, Michelle, and Jennifer for letting me use your real names. Sorry/ Not sorry that I had to kill you all off. At least you were all fairly likeable characters.

Thank you to Troy Cooper, who designed the cover of BreathTaken

Thank you to Genevieve Scholl, "Editor Eve," for tidying up everything in a presentable bow and making sure nothing slides through the cracks. **Any mistakes that have slipped through are entirely my own doing.**